To Ca... CW00859654

Alan,

Enjoy the ride
with love

Vatscha

20. 1. 2014

RUBIES AND
RICKSHAWS

Vatsala Virdee

Bloomington, IN Milton Keynes, UK

AuthorHouse™
1663 Liberty Drive, Suite 200
Bloomington, IN 47403
www.authorhouse.com
Phone: 1-800-839-8640

AuthorHouse™ *UK Ltd.*
500 Avebury Boulevard
Central Milton Keynes, MK9 2BE
www.authorhouse.co.uk
Phone: 08001974150

First published by AuthorHouse 2/14/2006

ISBN: 1-4208-8397-6 (sc)

Printed in the United States of America
Bloomington, Indiana

This book is printed on acid-free paper.

For my father, for changing worlds.

ACKNOWLEDGEMENTS

*R*ubies and Rickshaws started as a leap of faith which became a journey spanning several exciting years. I would like to thank all my friends, in particular, Michael Gerrard, for his technical expertise and unfailing belief in me, Andrei Dmitrichev, for his inspiration which meant so much, Cynthia Hammel, for her colourful contribution making the tough task of rewriting so much fun and my editor, Katharine Turok, whose guidance on various drafts of the manuscript carrried me to the very end. I wish to thank the Oza family for their support, my daughter, Natisha, for spearheading the marketing campaign, my son, Jasmeer, for his constructive and delightful feedback and my husband, Tejinder, for loving me.

www.rubiesandrickshaws.com
Website and design created by Michael Gerrard

www.sibleyphoto.com
Cover photograph by Kevin Sibley

Contents

I

Deception

"*I* don't love you," he groaned, lingering over each word and yet he kissed her with the warmth of the sun, as if she was the only woman he had ever cared for. She knew he loved her but could not bring himself to admit it. She also knew that with every touch of their lips he was losing her.

Words without meaning, she convinced herself, *I do not care.* They were words for the sake of speech, words of no consequence, words that could not speak for his heart nor look into his soul or capture the sweet unsaid nothings incised in his eyes. She tightened her firm hold around his hard body. Her grip imprisoned him in her canopied bed like a helpless creature in a lioness's den. This way he would be etched in her memory forever. She was glad – *glad* – they had never really made love. He would become her Rosetta stone, an ancient script revealing a rich and powerful heritage and this, she knew, would lead her to the path of discovery. He would become her dream catcher, a moment she would never forget, a past she would always remember and an emotion that would stay with her for the rest of her days.

"I don't believe what you say anymore," she retorted as she returned his kisses more earnestly, more passionately, when suddenly a powerful sense of loss came over her. Her heart raced out of control, she could hardly breathe. Her naked body began to sway in a compelling desire for fulfilment. With every agonizing moment she waited in vain for him to take her, she waited for him to prove he loved her.

3

She lifted her eyes and met his. When he did give her a glimmer of hope she felt betrayed by his sense of honour and integrity, his immeasurable capacity to love and his inability to tell her the truth.

Why is love so deceptive? she wondered, and chided herself for not defining the laws of love. Searching the past to justify the present, she made up her mind to leave Switzerland, her job and Alex Vadim, her first love, the only love she'd ever had in her twenty-three years.

"Tell me, Alex," she whispered, "How can I feel tenderness, passion, and rage and yet so much love for you?" He folded her into his arms and their lips pressed hungrily in a fierce embrace until one obstinate tear trickled down her cheek. She ran her fingers through his lustrous blond hair and cupped his face to hers. Her long hair reflected glints of dark indigo, making him think of the waves of the rapids under a half moon. Her radiant olive skin felt soft like virgin snow powder when he wrapped his right leg over her slender silhouette and his demanding hands pulled her closer. His fingers moved over her soft shoulders, he lifted one hand to trace the indentation of her spine and shapely buttocks, finally gripping her hips close to his. *How beautiful, soft and sexy,* he thought. *Her hair feels like silk, her scent like honeysuckle.* Gazing deeply into her dark almond eyes Alex changed register and kissed her tenderly on the forehead the way a mother would kiss her newborn child. And then, to her surprise, he began to lick away her saline tear. Alex gripped her more passionately until exhaustion triumphed, until they could move no longer, until the heat was too much, until tiredness overruled their love and lust for each other.

Alex fell asleep. She sat upright, her eyes wide open. She left the bed to study him, to practice distance. He was especially handsome in his half-naked elegance as she examined the emotional network of her love in perfect co-ordination with his. Lying in her bedroom, on her sheets, in her Swiss chalet, and locked in her heart, Alex was the epitome of shameless perfection.

As she turned toward the mirror, her long thick black hair tumbling over her shoulders, her nude body glistening in the moonlight, she saw the blurred reflection of a woman in love. Remembering Alex's masculine form pressing urgently against her, she began to imagine the moments they could have spent together. She imagined the feel of his alabaster-smooth skin against her trembling thighs. As her passion wove itself into a web of desire, she sat by the bedside and began to write for him, for her, for the times they had spent together.

How can I love a man who denies true love?

The warm night moved her to open the French windows beside her canopied bed, letting in the cool breeze. Alex stirred, shuddered, and stilled. With the silvery moon perched arrogantly in the distance, she succumbed to the harsh reality that their relationship was finally ending. *When had it started,* she wondered, her thoughts racing back two years to the Quarters Hotel in Kashmir. *Had his love ever been true? Had he truly cherished her as he would a delicate, fragrant red rose or simply an artificial one?*

Why do I burn for the attention of his heart?

The moon's luminous streaks spread like silver threads weaving through the calm waves of Lake St. Moritz, creating a stairway, a symbolic path of no return. Its light began to play tricks on a dream catcher, made of gold beads and white feathers, an old gift from Alex, still hanging in front of her window.

As she searched for some reassurance, she solicited even the moon's approval as she tried to make sense of her relationship with Alex and still hold onto her dreams. She continued writing.

What drives my passion only to suffer such anguish?
You do not love me and you do
You do not hate me and you do
I am everything as I am nothing
For I do not have any part of you
You conceal, you conceal

That is all I can feel
As I have never had a passion so strong
Nothing in my heart has lasted so long

Finally acknowledging their love had ended, she used her pen as the ultimate bearer of the last rites. With her adrenaline racing, she began to pen more of the truth and face confusing facts, painful facts. Feeling entirely alone, she poured her verse onto futile paper.

You disguise, you disguise.
You conceal and I confide
I look at you, pleading with you
To show me some compassion
As I am your woman
Your heart and your passion.

She meticulously folded her poem and put it into his worn brown leather jacket. Engulfed with a deep sense of loss as if she had been sent to the gallows, she prepared to leave. Nevertheless, she felt guilty for pushing him away and guilty for not telling him the truth about her past. She observed his slow, steady breathing oblivious of the hurt he must already be feeling. Shocked by her own inability to come clean, she decided nonetheless to leave him. But she knew she had no choice.

Carefully, so as not to disturb him, she slipped into a long satin gown. On a previous visit to St. Moritz, she had carefully placed, high on a ledge above the door, the key to the attic that she referred to as her private apartment. When she reached the top of the stairs leading to the apartment, her heart pounded. Stretching up on tiptoe, she found the key exactly where she had left it. A flood of moonbeams streamed into the room through the round glass window, illuminating the contents with iridescent light as she unlocked the door. Instantly, she felt that familiar elation at being on the brink of making a major decision. This time it would have to be the decision to go home.

The apartment, nestling directly under the sloping roof of the chalet, was just large enough for a sleigh bed and an adjacent shower room. The room could barely hold the large trunk, which had been tucked out of harm's way. The wooden door opened onto two steps, barely the width of a child's foot. Clouds of dust rose when she opened the trunk. She rummaged through its contents, until she found a gold box. It was the size of her hand, framed with tiny white rice pearls, which her father had given her the day she left home.

She opened it, smiled to herself, and closed the lid, tucking it away in her bag.

She stepped into the shower. The melody of the cascading waterfalls echoed in her thoughts. Her mind drifted further into a past she had deserted many years ago. *Now, with Alex out of my life*, she convinced herself, *I have to go back home, where I really belong. There's nothing here for me now.*

Slipping into blue jeans and a pink V-neck sweater and packing a few items, Paris Cassidis searched for her cameras. Especially her favourite Leica, it was still there and in fine shape. *How long had she had it?* She mused. Paris remembered purchasing it while working for Sidelines, an underground newsletter in Srinigar. She also spotted her new acquisition, the tiny digital camera, underneath it. She gathered her bags and locked the door, replacing the key where she found it. Paris made her way back down the stairs to Alex.

Opening the door to the bedroom, Paris delighted in his nude seductiveness in deep slumber and, just for a brief moment, she weakened in her resolve to leave him. Paris adored Alex, no matter how destructive this feeling could be, realising she knew, that at this very moment in time, she loved him without reservation. She would feel lost without him. She would feel empty without him. Paris had loved Alex too much, against any logic at all. Letting go of her bags, she went to him, and stood by the side of the bed. Before kissing him goodbye her fingertips reached out and traced a line along the left side of his perfect body. Paris tilted her head to gaze at his lips so full from the night's kissing. Then she puckered gentle kisses upon his feet, a mark of great respect, as a final tribute to their love and what it could have been. This was the man who had changed her life, the man who had lived by his honour, so true to his word, so dear to her heart, so loyal in friendship, and so trusting throughout their journeys together. As this part of Paris's life came to an end and the burden of regret began to overwhelm her again, she recalled the moments she and this maverick photographer had spent together, the moments of laughter, endearing friendship, and deep, yet unfulfilled love.

Quietly closing the door, Paris stepped out into the cool night air and looked up at the moon so full and bright appearing to float on water. She sighed with deep regret. *I wish I could keep him close to me … for just a while longer … she told herself, for just a while.* With tears welling, she left the chalet, hurt that he hadn't stirred when she had bid him farewell.

Just then, moved by the vibrations of her proximity and her fierce emotions, he turned and murmured into the empty room, "Paris, you know I do love you, I do. I love you, I do …"

Sutton Pearce grumbled as he began to shuffle his new deck of cards. The news of Paris's return to Cyber Media Solutions only to resign, had sent shock waves through the various communication networks and sparked gossip in the corridors of the vast open-plan offices based in Geneva. Paris's resignation had never been on his agenda. Just when he was under pressure to hang onto his key staff, he was losing the best he had ever had. With Paris gone and no one to replace her, Sutton felt defeated, frustrated that he had taken her too much for granted, even though she had been with CMS only two years.

The deck, firmly locked in his hands, was evenly split in two and set upright. The tip of his thumb hooked around one end, and the tips of his last three fingers hooked around the other. In an effort to focus and calm his nerves, he shuffled them with perfunctory rapidity. Tapping the bottom edge of each stack on the desk to plan his next move and even up the pack, he prepared to propel them into the basketball net.

The full-size basketball net had been rigged above his office door to discourage frantic personnel from charging in. Sutton began to catapult the cards simultaneously into the net with such momentum and speed that all fifty-two playing cards scored and landed like heavyweight feathers on the floor.

The door opened. Paris entered, wearing a fitted pair of blue jeans and a tiger-print tank top.

"What happened to the ball?" she teased, as Sutton opened his arms to greet her.

"I got caught out. Some oversized, overpaid, dinky, egocentric birdbrain walked in while I was free-throwing my best shot. It landed on his noggin' and knocked out the good-for-nothing ba ... !" He refrained from going into more detail. A short, stocky, dogmatic man, Sutton flashed his beady brown eyes at her and continued, "he threatened to sue, so we settled out of court. I quit throwing and he quit barging in. Thought cards would be a lot safer and turns out it's a lot more fun!"

Sutton's head resembled the ball tucked under his desk and his well-rounded stomach stirred her memories of childhood teddy bears. His foghorn voice evoked images of great maritime paintings showing searches for freighters lost in the dark. With his small feet, he kicked the cards aside. Normally a chatty character, the little man with a red face, wearing grey flannels and a loose-fitting tie around his partly unbuttoned blue shirt, got straight to the point.

"Paris, I need you in Kashmir. You've read the newspapers; you've listened to the news. Don't have to tell you why." Sutton cleared his throat and proceeded to tell her why. "I need you to cover the story. Your assignment here has ended and I've made arrangements for you to leave as soon as possible."

It was mostly lies, but he felt she was swallowing it and that he was doing a good job of bluffing. He was not going to give her up without a tug of war. Paris tried to interrupt but Sutton held up his hand and continued.

"But you're *not* resigning! I won't accept your resignation. You're on the payroll and there you'll stay until I say so! Is that understood?" he said, trying to sound as convincing as possible.

"You know you're impossible, Sutton. I've come here to say goodbye and you won't let me. You know I'm not coming back to CMS. It's crazy to pay me for nothing. I don't need the money. There's no guarantee that I'll work, particularly in the precarious situation that exists. As for getting back home to Kashmir, I'm not sure I *can!*"

Then Paris's complexion paled. Unexpectedly her voice lowered, and she told the truth behind her on-the-spot decision to leave.

"I've left Alex. It's over! I'm planning a few days in Agra with Kalpana before heading home."

"I'm sorry. I know how much Alex meant to you. Your call to the travel desk this morning sent me into one of my fits of despair. Never tell them a secret! They let the cat of the bag within two minutes of your hanging up!"

Paris gulped hard, trying not to burst into tears. Chewing on the edge of her lip, she quizzed Sutton.

"Has he been in touch?" she asked, hoping Alex had left a message.

"He's upset, Paris. Very! He wanted to see you. You should have told him you were leaving him! You said nothing, except for a poem you left in his pocket."

"So he mentioned it, did he?" she queried, feeling remorse.

"Yes, he did. What did you write?"

"It doesn't matter, Sutton. It's over and I'm going home."

"Well if that's what you want, I can't stop you, but I can send you on assignment and that's what I'll do. So when you get back home to Kashmir, hook up the cell phone and send me a message. You've got the digital camera, so use it! Just upload the images to your notebook, as many as you can. I'm interested in anything you've got to offer, but take care of yourself, don't get killed or kidnapped!" He threw her a knowing glance.

Her curiosity aroused, Paris asked, "Where's Alex now?"

"He's leaving for Baghdad! I had to send him with the rest of the team. You should have been with him … on assignment. You've let your team down Paris, but I understand, so I'm not going to hold it against you. He's the best I've got, besides you, and Alex knows how to look after himself. He'll come out in one piece."

Wearily eyeing the mess on the floor, Sutton began to come to terms with the realization that he might never see her again. Opening his arms to her, he tried to sound harsh.

"Now get out of here before I change my mind, I've got work to do!"

"Thanks Sutton, I'll always love you," Paris confessed as they hugged affectionately.

"I'll miss you Paris, you're the best. You're the most professional woman I've ever worked with." Sutton hesitated and then added. "And the most daunting, dazzling dame I've ever set my eyes on … now don't look at me like that … I know looks don't count, but there can be no two Parises, that's for sure. Stay in contact and keep your batteries charged!"

Sutton had always been a great one for words, but this time he felt incapable of finding the right ones. However, Paris noticed faint lines of sadness above his brow. It was obvious he did not wish to lose her. Sutton keeping her within the safety net of CMS lifted her spirits and eased the ordeal of her returning home without a job.

Paris made her way back to her office to clear it out and send a fax to The Cascades. The airline tickets were already lying on her desk along with a fax from Kalpana, which read, "Just got your message! Party Saturday night at The Abbey. I've booked us a table with Satish. Can't wait to see you after all this time! Why the sudden surprise visit?

Regards to Sutton and say a big hello to Alex. Is he coming with you? Dying to see you! Kalpana."

The morning papers had arrived earlier than usual. Sutton, who had been battling with the early morning news of Paris's return to Headquarters to resign, had not read the headlines. "Terror and Turmoil in India. Ethnic groups clash in vicious mayhem. Four hundred people perish in widespread violence. Train stopped and torched. Coaches filled with pilgrims burned. Crowds of innocent people set ablaze." He checked the time and called Alex.

Paris fastened her seat belt and prepared herself for the long journey home. She knew Alex would have called her if he could. Paris began to write poems for him, for her, for the good times, the bad times, and for the day when they had first met.

2

The Snow Leopards

$\mathscr{Y}$ears ago …

The Palace of Malamar lies engulfed in the thick brush of the Himalayan forest and north of the rising sun. This obscure corner of the Kashmir valley remains a mystery to most people as only a few have been able to penetrate its merciless terrain. Those who have managed the treacherous uphill climb to the palace have never disclosed its location, nor have they drawn a map of the area leading to the great gateway of the two pink stone elephants. The opulent structure, a fortress with pillars appearing to rise above the snowy peaks, was built to symbolize and preserve the ancient myths and glorious traditions of the Malamar dynasty. Its remoteness provided a haven for the wealth belonging to its royal family. The Palace of Malamar became a treasure trove of unimaginable riches waiting to be pillaged.

The little girl ran as fast as she could, as far as she could, to get away from the palace, going deep into the harsh treacherous forest which lay beyond the palace grounds, heading desperately for her hideout. She heard a storm of horses urged on by their marauding bandit riders, who carelessly hurtled through a flock of grazing sheep and sped toward the two stone elephants. The horses, which had broken into furious gallops, were escorted by a leap of captured snow leopards bounding like lightning through the familiar terrain. One opportunistic predator, whose rope gave way in the confusion, escaped. The leopard slaughtered a sheep and sank its teeth into its prey, dragging the carcass onto the steeper and more rugged cliff edge. The little girl fled.

The stampede of these nearly extinct cats, rounded up into captivity by the invaders, spurred on the little girl, and she finally scrambled for cover into a fallen tree trunk. She curled into a cocoon, her knees glued to her chin. Her body shivered as she waited in the muggy airless hole to be rescued. The fair hairs on her soft skin shot upright as she quivered with fear. Then came the ghostly echoes of butchery inflicted on her home. The ricocheting bullets deafened her senses and awakened a forest scavenger, a brown tawny eagle eager to feed off fresh prey. The noise sent golden leaf monkeys erratically fleeing in all directions while she sat inert, in the tree trunk, awaiting liberation, longing for her governess to find her.

The leafy branches concealed her hiding place which had taken her weeks of daredevil planning. During her clandestine escapades, when the palace staff had been too busy to take any notice of her, she had gone through the forbidden gateway of the pink elephants and fearlessly penetrated into the forest alone. One day the little girl had accidentally come upon a severed tree trunk large enough to serve as a hiding place. She planned to use it one day to baffle her governess. The little girl had enjoyed these secret moments of adventure beyond anything else she had known in her six innocent years. She loved the unknown, thrived on the unexpected, and felt proud whenever she sat alone undetected in the hollow of the tree she had painstakingly carved out herself.

Although her governess knew all the secret trails she usually played along, the little girl had not only left the palace undetected that day, but to confuse her governess, she'd decided to deliberately venture farther than usual, just for fun. The little girl knew that this time her governess would never find her.

Now the little girl, hidden in the trunk, craved freedom. She longed for her mother's comforting lap, her mother's kisses and her father's words of courage while she remained fearful and miserably alone. Huddled in her refuge, digging her body into the bark, a wave of nausea hit her stomach and she began to heave.

Meanwhile the invaders indulged in a savage show, creating mayhem on the palace grounds. While the two-foot tall snow leopards were skinned for their precious grey and creamy-black spotted fur coats, their blood flowing freely in streams, the bandits rounded up the men and women and divided them into groups. The once pristine marble palace courtyard had now taken on the appearance of a slaughterhouse. Women were beaten until they crumpled to the ground and their young daughters were raped in front of their fathers. The older women were brutalized; their lifeless bodies piled high onto the heap of butchered snow leopards. Some men were bound and forced to watch. Husbands and fathers begged for mercy to no avail. Wailing children were silenced with bullets. Elders were lined against a wall and shot in the head with a single round. The entire slaughter took barely an hour to perform. While some of the murderers sacked the palace residence, others pillaged the dead bodies, finishing off anyone still alive. Miraculously the golden throne, weighing more than one hundred and twenty kilos, buried under several layers of superb wedding silks, remained majestically untouched, undetected in the centre of the palace courtyard. The royal family of the Palace of Malamar had once lived and now had died.

3

Angels and Waterfalls

$\mathscr{A}$long the lake of Surinsar, the palace can rarely be glimpsed by the humble houseboat vendors gliding listlessly along the serene waters. It is only at dawn, as the sun peeps out over the horizon, the palace sometimes sparkles in the distance as the sunlight reflects its powerful rays onto the lake. However, the entire image of the palace can be seen while gazing into the water as if searching for a three-dimensional image. The pillars appear to multiply in the ripples of this natural rainwater reservoir. The palace is often mistaken for the snowy peaks of the Himalayas. One aspect that clearly distinguishes it from the snow-capped mountains is its dazzling shades of lavender, mauve and purple.

The approach to Malamar starts in the foothills of the valley of Lake Surinsar, where a narrow slope hugs the river Tawi as it flows down into the valley. Pathways leading to Malamar are shrouded by gigantic conifers. As one loses sight of the calm waters of Lake Surinsar with its profusion of lotus flowers, migratory birds, Siberian ducks and swimming waterfowl, one enters the beguiling wilderness.

Upon arriving in the valley in the company of two sure-footed mules, a middle-aged doctor, Nachiketa came to a standstill beside the lake. The warm temperatures and blue cloudless skies prompted him to scan the undulating water. A direct gleam, accompanied by a path of shadows, directed his eyes until the lake became a mirror of dancing sunbeams. Nachiketa was distracted by a couple of houseboat vendors standing precariously on the edge of their boats and staring

into the water. *Had they seen the palace?* he asked himself.
If the palace was there, he would be able to find the path
leading to the Nathiyan cave temples. He examined the lake
again until the pillars came into sight. He blinked to clear
his eyes, sharpening the vision. Adjusting his sight several
times until the three-dimensional pillars were undisputedly
in view, he tried to inspect the sky but its luminosity blinded
him. Again, Nachiketa focused his eyes until the palace
appeared one more time, confirming what he had already
suspected that the legend of Malamar was true. Wiping the
perspiration from his brow, he splashed himself with the
glacial lake water in sheer exultation. He hugged his loyal
mules and led them to the lake to drink. His heart raced as
he made his calculations. Nachiketa's dream had come true
but there was no time to waste. The good weather was excuse
enough to set off to find the palace and then the trail that
would lead him to the cave temples. Without further delay,
as the morning sun settled, Nachiketa headed for the hills.

For sometime, Nachiketa had been travelling alone by
foot, in the company of his two mules, while meditating
on the teachings of the great Sadhu Swami. His destination was the famous pink granite cave temples of Nathiyan,
fifty-seven miles northwest of the city of Jammu, where
his beloved guru had achieved enlightenment. The temples
were etched into a cliff face, among meadows of blue poppies, high up on the windswept mountain peaks. This was
Nachiketa's ultimate goal - to reach the cave temples and
receive a blessing for a child, by paying respects to his most
revered One.

His firm aim was to ask the gods to bless his childless
marriage with a child. With this in mind, walking in a

northerly direction, he continued to follow a narrow lane, blushing with cherries, leading approximately to the spot where he had predicted his trail should begin.

The lake disappeared from view as he moved away from Surinsar. Treading carefully, he led the mules, resting them hourly and read from Tagore's *Gitanjali,* a book of magical early 20th-century poems often referred to as songs. Nachiketa, a man with a free spirit and deep faith, was a quiet man. He was well versed in the teachings of Hindu Dharma, and a pundit of languages including English, which he had taught himself from discarded textbooks. Diminutive, with shoulder-length greying hair, luminous eyes full of wisdom and grey bushy eyebrows, he was bundled up in several warm black woollen sweaters and coarse coffee-coloured overalls belted around the waist. Following the uphill track through clumps of dusky pink heather and evergreens, he entered the forest along the outskirts of the giant conifers, where he discovered an overgrown maze and a vast cluster of ancient bo trees. Clearing the jumble of tangled shrubs, he found another path and guided his mules for some time, hearing the river Tawi crashing long before it came into view. The midday sun's rays were about to reach the valley, when he saw, in the not-too-far distance, the stately pillars of the Palace of Malamar.

"Could anything more extraordinary exist?" Nachiketa exclaimed to his mules, stroking them soothingly as the palace came into view. He could feel its spirit, its majestic presence, and the great civilization it represented. The pillars appeared to be floating on a bed of light. This marble splendour intermittently changed colour from lavender to mauve, mauve to blue, blue to purple and then turned to pink, yellow, orange and finally red, the colour of passion, the colour of love.

When the sounds of gunshots and pounding hooves no longer filled the air, the little girl decided to make her escape down the valley and into town, a place she had never visited. As she climbed out of the tree, her soft skin scraped against the jagged strips of dry wood and began to sting.

Nearby, a stray snow leopard was sniffing out its next prey. Upon seeing the animal from afar, his long lush tail and gleaming eyes, the little girl screamed and darted for the river. Robed in fine scarlet silk, she pulled her golden organza shawl over her head to distract the leopard already in hot pursuit. She sprinted more and more deeply into the forest. As she ran, she slipped several times, lost her golden sandals, and ripped her scarlet silk skirt, as her long raven locks flew in the wind behind her. The leopard heavily padded paws gripped the ground firmly as it tracked her with tireless energy and unrelenting force. Finally, her golden organza shawl twisted around her feet, tripping her up on a bed of pebbles, setting off a miniature landslide. Stealing away on the blanket of gravelled dirt, clutching her golden organza shawl, she dived over the cliff, where she vanished. A few critical seconds later the little girl's shawl, tangled around her ankle, snagged precariously on a twig. Suspended for several seconds with one leg in the air, the other scraped against the cliff edge as it dangled haphazardly over the side. She swayed back and forth until the thorns gradually ripped through the delicate gold thread.

Just inches away from the doctor's head, she fell, toppling him over as she hit the ground.

Suddenly tumbling from the sky like an angel into the gardens of Shalimar, the little girl landed at Nachiketa's feet, knocking him over with a heavy thud. *Why have the gods opened the skies so soon?* He wondered, flabbergasted, as a girl lay numb and unmoving at his feet. Quickly examining her for broken bones and head injuries, he could make out her faint heartbeat. She has been fleeing! *But why and from whom?* Fearful of the unknown, he carefully positioned her on one of his mules and waded through the icy water of the river, along a ravine, until he came upon an inlet behind a waterfall. Dragging his shivering mules into it, he tied them up and left them to rest. After swathing the girl in a thick woollen blanket to keep her as dry and warm as possible, he bathed her head to stop the swelling on her face. Bandaging her wounded leg, he built a small fire.

As she slept, he waded back upstream to the same spot he had found her, and then climbed uphill along the beaten track in the direction of the palace. A huge griffon vulture, appearing remarkably graceful in flight with broad dark wings, swooped dangerously close and then soared into the bluest of skies. Challenged by the intimidating forest, Nachiketa defiantly used his staff to sweep aside the underbrush at the foot of the cliff. Then he climbed the steep and slippery rock face by transferring his slight weight onto the protruding branches and using them as hand and foot holds, when suddenly another griffon vulture swooped by almost knocking him off. Holding tightly onto one branch with one hand, and by swift, sudden movements of his staff, he fought the vulture off. Never losing sight of the palace pillars, he reached the base of the giant conifers. Nachiketa calculated that should he continue in a northerly direction, he would come upon the palace. The sky was now swarming with sinister vultures gliding effortlessly on gigantic wings. Carrying a heap of bones, they began to drop them randomly from immeasurable heights. Nachiketa planted his staff at the top of the cliff, pinpointing his route back to the inlet, and then proceeded to find the palace.

An expanse of ancient banyan trees joined by long aerial roots lined the route. The roots spread over the trunks and branches. This had created extensive thickets that he painstakingly brushed aside as he struggled on. Hulking vultures, with their colossal wings folded, were nesting in crags and tall pine trees. While vigilantly eyeing their foreboding bare heads as well as their powerful curved beaks, Nachiketa took refuge among the thickets. The predators, proudly displaying their powerful talons, soared and circled above him. They landed nearby in pairs, tearing to pieces the carcass of a dead sheep that had been partially devoured just moments before by the formidable snow leopard. The vultures feasted on their delicious prey as they squawked at a bevy of screeching birds desperate to join in the binge.

As the banyan trees fell behind, two lavish pink stone elephants greeted him. Their soft and smiling faces put him at ease. It was, he would reflect years later, as if the elephants were welcoming him into their world, a strange land, a land of paradise, of unimaginable wealth, a haven untainted, untouched and unattainable to most. Their splendour and their majestic appearance mesmerized him. At first glance the elephants looked larger than the palace. Their salmon-pink bodies were elaborately bejewelled in ceremonial attire and the gates in the distance looked minuscule in comparison.

As Nachiketa walked toward the stone elephants, he came across the emerald carpets of grassy lawns, shaven and weeded to resemble the mosses which grew abundantly in small batches along the river. The flowerbeds edging the lawns were decorated with blooms he had never seen. Purple cornflowers, red trumpet vines laced with groups of violet and pink foxglove delighted him, as he paused to pluck a few red trumpets. Some moments later, as he arrived in the main courtyard, the flowers he had been carrying dropped from his grasp when he saw the bloodbath. Nachiketa lost his balance as his knees buckled in disbelief. Eventually he tried to move, feeling overwhelmingly inert as he tripped over several blood-soaked bodies, causing him to cry out in terror. Although a doctor for many years, all too familiar with the sights and smells of death, these hideous murders sickened him. Nachiketa courageously forged ahead to search for the girl's family, becoming increasingly nervous in the sinister silence. A huge fountain in the centre of the courtyard ran blood red as ravaged corpses intermingled with the sliced-up remains of snow leopards. White marble screens carved with hundreds of lotus flowers, and used as a façade to protect shy ladies of the court, were splashed red. The marble pillars, rising taller than the ancient pillars of Persepolis, which lined the pathway to the pleasure gardens of the Malamar court, had been ravaged by bullets. Nachiketa felt the eerie silence of senseless death ever more intensely. He saw the evil handiwork of the devil himself. While the vultures' menacing cries rang out overhead, Nachiketa vomited violently.

Then Nachiketa heard some scuffling noises, scarcely audible. He glanced furtively sideways and spotted a young woman, her shredded sari bloodstained, moving into view from behind a pillar. Blood trickled from her mouth. He went to her side and held her in his arms, administering drops of water from his flask. "Young woman, please tell me how I can ease your pain," Nachiketa pleaded.

"My daughter," she sobbed, "please go and find her … she is playing in the forest. My daughter is playing hide and seek. Take care of her … give her our blessing … give her your home. There's no one left except for the prince …".

"Young woman," he beseeched, "where is the prince? I see no prince here."

"He ran … like a tiger … I tried to save him … he took shelter under the throne. I begged him … to leave … to go to the cave temples … please … my humble friend, I beg you … find them and give them your home."

As she gasped for breath, Nachiketa dried her tears, wiped away the blood and lifted her head to ease the pain. The young woman continued to implore him, faintly.

"Follow the river until you come to a path pointing to the midday sun … from there the river forks … and a garden of yellow cinquefoils begins. Here … you will you find another trail … sunflowers … rope bridge … leading to the caves … not more than a day's walk … please go …". The young woman's voice trailed off and she revealed what she had been hiding behind her back.

Clutched in the young woman's hand was a breathtaking necklace studded with knuckle-size red rubies and precious diamonds set in gold. A multitude of sparkling pavé diamonds rimmed the necklace. Its fastener was a two-inch gold pin. The jewels cascaded down in chains forming a long V-shape. The necklace's sheer weight and magnificence dazzled him.

"Take this necklace." the young woman begged him. "It is part of their heritage, their birthright, their ancestry. It will give them the courage to begin again here in our native land ... when they return ... they should return."

She gasped for breath as she struggled to disclose the mysteries of Malamar. Tears of bitterness and loss streamed from her eyes as the young woman stammered her last words. Nachiketa stayed by her side listening, trying to understand her every wish.

At last her body became limp and her lifeless head fell against his shoulder. *The young woman who had fallen into life's longest sleep and drifted into the unknown, to be born again a purer spirit, now embraced her new life.* Nachiketa thought. In the wake of her death he was left to pick up the pieces, rescue the children and give them a home.

As dusk fell, he left the palace through the bloody courtyard. Nachiketa made his way back into the forest by way of the banyan trees and came across the mangled remains of sheep. The vultures had disappeared and the forest had become eerily silent again. Racing back, he came across his staff marking the way back to the inlet. A few minutes later, he was clambering down the steep rock formation and into the river, wading back along the route to the inlet. The sleeping little girl appeared not to have moved while he had been away.

Nachiketa was unable to contain his grief. He was a man of great faith, but nothing had quite prepared him for this. And yet now he was suddenly the sole guardian of a parentless child on this journey to the cave temples of Nathiyan. This nameless little girl, he reflected, who today had become an orphan in the most brutal manner, whose land had been pillaged, whose family had been wiped out by Yama, The God of Death, was now in his care. For the first time in his life he began to doubt his own faith. *How can God reward me in this way,* he tormented himself. *How can He grant me my wish for a child in such a fashion? How can I merit such a precious gift from such painful circumstances?* As the evening sky blackened, he beckoned Yama and asked him why he taken so many lives. Nachiketa reasoned with him. He scolded him. He fought with him and finally accepted him, reluctantly at first but, as the early morning light appeared on the distant horizon, he settled his score with him. Nachiketa, holding his head high, found the courage and strength to move on with his life in the way that he believed God wanted. So as the morning dew glistened around him and the little girl slept peacefully, he made up his mind to rescue the boy.

Now the journey had become urgent. However, to make the trip with an injured child was too risky unless he could find a silk-cotton tree with its rare medicinal properties. After dismissing the idea of taking the little girl down to Surinsar for medicines, he decided to go after the boy, provided he could find the tree. Nachiketa considered that if he could extract the tree's rare salve, said to be secreted from bees, the little girl would recover swiftly enough for them to follow the trail, which was less than a day's walk away, according to the young woman who had lain dying in his arms. To find the tree with its healing properties was the only way to begin the journey.

Well before dawn the next day, Nachiketa trudged into the forest until he heard the buzzing of thousands of bees. He continued in its direction until he came upon a silk-cotton tree. He decided to build a fire at the bottom of its enormous trunk and went in search of leaves to feed it. As the fire began to smoulder, it sent dense columns of smoke up through the massive branches of the tree to distract the bees away from their hives. Preparing his torch, a stick wrapped with leaves and vines which honey hunters burn to drive bees away, Nachiketa began to climb the gargantuan tree.

Gripping his torch in one hand he scrambled up the tree, covering his face and neck with a thick shawl for protection against the ferocious bee stings. As he climbed the trunk, and the smoke rose, the buzz escalated to a vicious hum. Easing his way onto a narrow branch, he confronted the bees with his smouldering torch. The first hive hung like a massive melon, with scores of smaller beehives nestling well above it in the branches. As Nachiketa balanced on a branch, clouds of angry insects filled the air. Then, as he waved his torch to distract the bees, he was stung on the hand while cutting away a large chunk of milky white wax studded with bee larvae. Pain shot through his arm as other bees tried unsuccessfully to fling themselves into his face. Protected somewhat by the smoke from his torch, he hauled the wax quickly down to the ground. His fingertips were numb from the painful sting and his legs were shaking.

Feeling light-headed, he sat down by the fire and began to pull out the sting with a sharp needle shaped like an arrow. Then, without a moment to spare, he prepared a batch of honey salve from the pollen and wax. Nachiketa removed a chunk to use as food later and hastily returned to the inlet.

Rallying back to the shelter where the girl lay with his mules, Nachiketa massaged her swellings with the salve. He cooked breakfast, fed his mules and waited for her to show signs of life. He fed her drops of honey slowly. As the early morning rays of light streamed into the inlet, her eyes opened and she began to cry hysterically at the sight of Nachiketa squatting at the entrance. When she saw the mules next to him, she stopped abruptly, fascinated, and then continued to watch as Nachiketa drank a cup of hot tea. He was grateful for the special honey which had not only revived her but had numbed the smarting pain in her legs and reduced the swelling on her forehead to a small and inconsequential bump.

"Would you like to eat, my little one? I have honey and eggs to bring you back to life and build your strength. Perhaps a drink of hot tea to keep you warm?"

The little girl sat upright, her almond eyes open wide, her long raven hair flowing around her shoulders, and stammered, "Who are you? Where's my mother? Where are we?" before bursting into tears again.

"My name is Keta, I found you in the forest … don't cry … I won't hurt you … I'm here to help you. Tell me, little one, do you remember your name?" he replied patiently.

"I don't know! I don't know and if I did I would not tell you!" she retorted courageously. "Where are my parents … my family … my governess … the prince … the prince … I *always, always* play with the prince … where's my family?" she demanded sobbing. "I want to go home! … I want my mother … my mother … where is she?" she screamed, as if Nachiketa were a million miles away.

"Do you not remember your name, little one? If not, I will call you Angel," he told her gently.

"I'm trying … I'm trying … I'm trying so hard to remember … I'm trying so hard … but I can't remember … I was running in the forest and then I fell and now my head hurts and my leg hurts. Who are you? Why am I here? Why … why … why have you brought me to this horrible cold place?" she insisted, as tears streamed down her face, searching his for an answer.

"You fell from the skies, and I brought you here to keep you warm," he explained cryptically.

"I don't want to be warm … I want my mother … Where's my mother?" she moaned, crawling into a corner and burying her head in her lap. Nachiketa stayed put.

"I do not know," he lied, protecting her.

"And my father … Has my father sent you to take me home? Where's my father … my father would never leave me here … Did he send you to take me home?" she demanded, sobbing again.

"I cannot say … but I know they love you very much. Now you must stay with me until we find the prince. I will look after you. I will feed you. I will be your eyes and ears on this journey. I will be a shoulder for all your burdens. I will carry you when you tire. I will be your humble servant. If you are hungry, I will feed you. If you wish to bathe, then I will take you to the river. If you want me to read to you, then I will read to you. I will be your guardian. I will watch over you. I will obey you, little one. Tomorrow we will go together to the Nathiyan temple. The prince will be there.

Now … I only ask you to rest. You must be strong for the journey. You must eat and you must drink hot tea. Do not be afraid. I will protect you."

"I don't want to rest. I want to go home," she insisted, clutching onto her gold organza shawl. "Why don't you answer my questions? I demand that you answer *all* my questions! Did my father send you? Where is my mother? I demand that you take me home now!" she commanded, standing up, throwing her shawl to the ground, and straightening her torn skirt. "I shall travel on one of your mules!" she announced, resolutely brushing her hair aside with her small hand, tilting her chin slightly.

According to traditional beliefs, the Nathiyan cave temples were carved by the gods only some centuries ago. It is rumoured that should anyone be so fortunate as to find them, they would be blessed with a child. Life would become a passage into another world where possessions would have no importance and all life forms would be treated in the same manner, with love and respect.

Although there are no maps to follow or guides to lead the way, common knowledge suggests that the entrance to the cave temples are located inside a ravine. The ravine is precariously positioned at the end of the valley, halfway under a peak, shaped like an eagle. The journey through the Himalayan valley is striking and the path is strewn with blue poppies, a flower the colour of the sky at dawn. These poppies droop slightly when wide open. They are so fragile that their petals drop off at the slightest touch protected only by the sharp spines arranged on the stem and buds. To arrive at the path of the poppies, one should follow the Tawi river until the water tastes as sweet as honey. It is only then that the shadows of the day will lift and the granite cave temples will appear.

The next day, after the little girl awoke well before the morning sun, nothing would console her. Nachiketa hastily gathered up his belongings and seated her atop one of his mules. With no time to waste, they followed the river until it divided. Then they took the path leading to the clumps of yellow cinquefoils which they had spotted in the distance. With the tearful little girl on mule-back refusing to talk and he on foot, they journeyed until the sun began to set and the first shadows of night began to fall. Drinking from the river, they at last stumbled onto a brook where the water appeared to taste sweet.

Overcome with joy, Nachiketa continued on, hoping to find the young prince. They came to the fragrant meadow full of blue poppies when suddenly the evening shadows lifted and the pink granite cave temples appeared. The little girl, who had remained silent during the journey, decided to walk the rest of the way, now desperate to find the prince. Nachiketa extended his hand to help her down and she, tilting her dignified head, accepted.

They waded hurriedly together, hand in hand, like father and daughter through knee-deep blooms and foliage. The valley floor was covered with an array of white bell-shaped campanula. As the young dying woman had predicted, sun-flowers led them to a rocky stretch laced with pink anemo-nes near a rope-bridge. The little girl, her legs aching, now insisted on being carried, so Nachiketa hauled her up onto his skinny shoulders and carried her over to the right bank of the river. They spotted the ravine precariously positioned at the end of the valley below a peak, shaped like an eagle. Though still in the distance, they could see the faraway entrance to the cave temples and the uphill path leading to them.

Nachiketa's prayers had finally been answered. He had found the cave temples. This was the land of miracles and miracles were fast becoming a part of his life. *Had not the angel of God, who had fallen from the skies, been a miracle?* he contemplated. *She had been a gift, a sign, a marvel, a supernatural phenomenon. Had God planned it this way?* he asked himself. Nachiketa now wondered whether the little girl had been his guide along this spiritual path, which had ultimately led him to the cave temples. *And what of the prince*, he mused, *would he be there?*

The cave temples were a symphony of stone. One major scene depicted the life of Lord Shiva energetically creating the world with a cosmic dance. The symbolic fertility temple, the most sensual one of all, was an immense cave temple flanked by two snow leopards and their cubs. Inside Nachiketa saw images carved out of solid rock illustrating court life in all its pomp. Sensuous dancers, richly bejewelled alongside gem-ornamented princes and voluptuous, slim-waisted princesses, were copiously depicted in a variety of poses, loving each other in erotic moments.

Nachiketa sat down crossed-legged with the dignified little girl. The silence was golden, the air pure, their breath calm and the spirit peaceful. With their hearts stable, their souls at peace, nirvana was imaginable. Here he prayed to Saraswati, the goddess of endurance, learning and wisdom, for the prince's safety. He prayed to Surya, the sun god, the source of life, for the prince's survival. He prayed to Mahadevi, the great mother goddess, for a child of his own. Nachiketa prayed until dusk overcame them and the night sky shrouded them in darkness while they waited in vain for the young prince to appear.

The next day, the little girl began to learn the ways of the Hindu gods. It was at the cave temples, under the guidance and teachings of Nachiketa when she began to understand the meaning and origins of the Hindu Dharma. It was also at the cave temples that she began to appreciate the world's oldest living religion. The little girl learned tolerance, resilience, and the need for peace.

Seven days passed without a sign of the young prince. During that time, Nachiketa comforted the little girl with fairytales and nursery rhymes. From time to time he performed magic tricks to lift her spirits. Then, he educated her from dawn to dusk, enchanting her with funny stories, fables, proverbs and poems.

"Hindus believe there are no heathens and no enemies. They believe in non-violence. They believe that everyone has a right to evolve spiritually and realize the truth in time." Too young to understand the significance, the little girl memorized his words and he sensed her rapt attention. Nachiketa continued, "Hindus believe in reincarnation, which means that we have many lives until one has reached liberation. One is responsible for all actions through the law of Karma."

Nachiketa recounted fables about the law of being, the path of righteousness, religion, duty, responsibility, virtue, goodness and truth. The little girl absorbed all the education he willingly passed on. He taught her about the origins of old civilizations, the evidence of Hindu astronomers mapping the constellations, doctors performing surgery and scholars writing the ancient books.

"Build the mind, not just the muscles," Nachiketa would tell her, "mould the spirit not just the surroundings, increase your worth through your inner spirit and not through wealth and power."

"Please tell me who you are! What does Nachiketa mean?" The little girl asked one day.

"My dearest young and innocent child, Nachiketa lived in the Vedic era thousands of years ago. Once, when he saw his father sacrifice weak withered cows during a spiritual ceremony, Nachiketa volunteered to be sacrificed. Angry, his father cursed him and offered him to Yama, The God of Death instead."

"But why would a father give his own child away, why?" She was puzzled thinking of her own father, knowing he would never give her away. Suddenly she wondered when her father would come to take her home. For a fleeting moment, from the back of her mind, she heard screams of terror coupled with the terrifying echoes of bullets coming from the palace grounds. Then the little girl wondered whether her parents were really still alive.

Nachiketa continued. "Listen, my little one, listen." he replied, gently scolding her for her impatience. "Anger invites the devil. It makes us behave foolishly and irrationally. The child found himself at the doors of death all alone but he remained fearless, waiting three days without food or rest. When Yama arrived he was pleased by the child's bold determination and so granted him three wishes. Nachiketa's third wish was for knowledge of the soul. It would mean victory over death. Therefore, Yama, in order to trick him, tried to tempt Nachiketa with offers of wealth, kingdoms, maidens and other luxuries of the universe. But the child remained unmoved. Nachiketa's firm aim earned him Ultimate Spiritual Knowledge."

"Tell me more?" she pleaded. "Does this mean if I have a firm aim, my dreams will come true?" the little girl asked, desperate to find a way to bring her family back to life again, knowing that they might well be dead. "Tell me, what does this all mean. Tell me, explain everything to me."

"A child whose aim is firm can move the world. Aim focuses our energies and generates great strength and courage. It produces a special fearlessness that can challenge all trials and temptations. At times, it can even defy death. However, my young and inquisitive little girl, aim is not enough. You must have a good aim, an aim that uplifts oneself as well as the whole of humanity."

On the seventh day before dusk, when the prince had still not appeared, the little girl cried until she fell asleep exhausted. Nachiketa squatted by the fire in reflection, wondering how she was going to deal with the death of her parents. They had waited seven long days for the prince, but now, with a heavy heart, he knew he would have to break his promise to the young dying woman at the palace and leave the cave temples at dawn. The gods had not answered all of his prayers, but he had faith that one day the prince would be found. With this in mind, he decided to take the little girl to Sambara, a village beyond the Surinsar wall, more than a hundred miles away.

Nachiketa prepared to take the six-year-old child home to his wife Seetha.

4

The Palace Hotel

From the tea lounge of the Palace Hotel in Montreux, offering the finest views of the snowy peaks of the Dents-du-Midi in the Alps, Jovi looked visibly perturbed as he scrutinized the magazine he was reading. From his waistcoat he pulled out his spectacles and looked more closely at the pictures.

"Jovi, tell me, what's so intriguing, my darling. I want to know everything!" uttered the pretty young woman who sat at his side. She smiled affectionately and slipped her arm into his, pulling him closer.

"It's nothing, my dear," he answered giving a shrug.

She looked at him inquisitively.

"Come now, you're not being honest. I've seen that look before. You've seen something to put you out of sorts. Tell me what it is! You know I'm the closest to your heart," she claimed with total conviction.

Jovi looked up at her and smiled. *Of course she is,* he thought. She grew lovelier every day and being in her company was a joy. To take care of the woman he had known all his life, had been his life. Her innocence was so overpowering, so alluring, that he found it impossible to remove her from his mind. She was part of him and there was nothing that he could do to change that.

She glanced at the magazine pictures and whispered coquettishly, "She's pretty, isn't she?"

"Yes," Jovi said sheepishly.

"She's familiar. I've seen her somewhere before." She looked up at Jovi, studying his anxious expression. "What is it, you look pale, are you getting sick?"

"No, I'm fine, but look at the pictures. Can't you see anything unusual?"

"She's striking, that's all I can see. A movie star perhaps?"

Jovi looked at her and laughed.

"You know you are the most adorable woman I've ever known."

She laughed, got up, tugged at his hand and said, "Come on, let's have some fun. I've booked a show in Lausanne and we'll eat dinner together in Vevey. A table for two, it's already booked!"

Jovi tore the pages from the magazine and put them into his pocket. Drawn by her potent charm, he got up to follow her. "Take my hand and lead the way, my gorgeous princess," he teased, "to the end of the world, if you like." They left leisurely, arm in arm.

Jovi's presentation on architecture at the Le Corbusier School in Montreux had been a success. The influential annual gathering had been an excuse to get back to Europe. After studying architecture in Switzerland for almost five years, he was now 25 years old and had returned to India permanently, travelling throughout the Indian states, lecturing in digital design and architectural art forms. He had also become well known in Europe, particularly in the tightly knit circles of New Age architects who were emerging in the West. With his first endeavour, The Cascades, a hotel in Agra, he had fulfilled his dream.

Jovi had become particularly interested in preserving derelict buildings, transforming them into habitable structures that expressed a sense of space coupled with high-level efficiency. Taking into account the current advances in architectural thought, his goal represented tranquillity, which was much in demand. With his novel designs, avant-garde approach and personal appreciation for cutting-edge style and innovations, he set up Dream Machines, his own thriving company.

With Dream Machines, he also adapted his ideas by turning structures of great historical significance into modern, environmentally-friendly buildings. Jovi believed in innovative technology within the boundaries of historical appreciation. He was convinced the mix could work and proved it by taking the ailing Metropolis Hotel in Agra, which he recreated as The Cascades. He had received recognition despite the odds and was the speaker of the moment, the man who set the pace in modern architecture. Jovi's ideal was to resurrect dreams. For this reason, in the architectural world he was called "Jovi the dream machine."

After the show they ate supper, but his mind was elsewhere, buried in the past. Jovi tried to be witty and amusing, but he knew he was doing a very bad job of it. He couldn't get the magazine photographs out of his mind. When the meal ended, he insisted on indulging in a cigar before retiring for the night. He sat alone in the tea lounge studying the pictures.

The article was titled "A Portrait of Paris." There were pictures of the famous CMS photojournalist, Paris Cassidis, in Kandahar and Herat in Afghanistan. Pictures showed her hugging a frail, pregnant woman shivering from the bitter cold, a sobbing 4-year-old son at his mother's side. In Liberia and Sierra Leone, the images showed Paris taking photos between gunfire and grenades. As he read on, the pictures revealed children whose families had been brutally murdered by the military. The article told the macabre story of what these vulnerable adolescents had been subjected to as they were recruited by the army at gunpoint. Teenagers marched in the streets hugging rifles and bayonets, while others held onto Paris's hand. They would never know, it went onto say, the pleasures of growing up in a family or of being loved. They had become robots in a war they could not understand. Learning to kill without remorse, life had no meaning for them. More photographs showed Paris working with the humanitarian aid agencies and, in particular, with the UN refugee agency in the Herat refugee camp.

A photograph of Paris donning a helmet and shouldering her cameras intrigued him. Her long dark hair blowing away from under her helmet and into the wind sent goose pimples up his spine. *Could this woman be a carbon copy of the woman in the painting hanging on his wall?* He had to find out. It was late but he called CMS.

"Cyber Media Solutions, can I help you?" shrilled the operator.

"Yes, I'm trying to track down one of your photographers, Paris Cassidis." He hesitated, expecting an unhelpful response. When he didn't get one he continued.

"It's a personal matter. Do you know how she can be contacted?" Jovi asked chewing on his cigar. He stubbed it out and held his breath.

"Paris Cassidis left on reassignment this morning. She's no longer based in Switzerland."

"Where can I contact her?" he said, feeling panic set in.

"One moment, sir." Jovi waited as the seconds turned to minutes.

"Kashmir, she's been reassigned to Kashmir. I have her travel plans on my database. Geneva-Agra."

Jovi fell silent.

"May I be of further assistance?"

"Er ... no, thanks, and thanks for the info."

"You're welcome," and the line went dead. The telephone remained pasted to his ear. Jovi went to his room to log onto his notebook computer and connect into the main network server for The Cascades hotel in Agra. After requesting an upload of all reservations for the coming two weeks, he poured himself a gin and tonic to calm his nerves and then proceeded to pace up and down the room in anticipation.

It was a long shot but he took a chance and began to filter the data, searching for Cassidis until he found her reservation for three nights. Jovi took a deep breath and closed his eyes, imagining the sweet fragrance of her youthful body and the image of her unusual beauty.

With no time to spare, Jovi rearranged Paris's reservation, booking her into the Mirabai Suite. Attaching her new booking details to his email, Jovi addressed it to the General Manager. Soon after, he phoned Geneva airport and booked seats to New Delhi. With tickets for himself and his companion, he was going home.

5

Love and Destiny at the Taj Mahal

As the plane landed in New Delhi and the cabin doors opened, the stifling heat burrowed its way through the air vents and besieged Paris. As she descended the stairwell, she began to long for the cool breezes flowing through the valleys of Sambara.

After checking into her hotel Paris decided to explore the city. She hailed a passing rickshaw and headed for the old quarter of Delhi. Along the way she bought an assortment of green and yellow oranges at a stall on the pavement just inches from the frenzied traffic. Circulating with locals from a collection of backgrounds entertained her and she chatted easily with gibbering vendors. In particular she was distracted by a red-turbaned Rajput performing a musical puppet show for a group of rambunctious children. As the hubbub intensified, merging with adventure, she knew she had become a prisoner of her own decision to return to India. Going home was like going back to the way she used to live.

Veiled women walked alongside others heavily decorated in showy jewels. Paris caught sight of a pompous-looking millionaire reclining in his spanking clean, chauffeur-driven black car. This man in Gucci sunglasses gazed out the slit of an open, tinted window at weary, skinny females bearing loads of bricks on their heads. Walking away from the rickshaw, Paris came across a chaotic queue of people buying tickets for the latest movies.

The next day, thinking about Alex, wondering where he was and how he was coming to terms with her sudden and inexplicable departure, she caught the early morning train to Agra which, to her surprise, was departing on time. With just moments to spare she jumped on, only to find that her reserved seat had been taken by a petite elder journeying to visit her lawyer grandson. After seeing that their tickets did indeed reserve the same seat, Paris, weighed down with cameras, left to find a free seat in another compartment.

A man wearing a starched white cloth folding into pleats at his waist, was snacking on green mangoes. He greeted Paris in the second-class compartment and made room for her. Paris sat by the window and closed her eyes, trying to shut out the world around her, trying to remember every detail of her last night with Alex and how it could have been if he'd made love to her. Paris wondered if she had made the right decision to leave Alex. She convinced herself that a visit to Kalpana was an excellent idea. *How perfect,* she reflected, *I'll visit the Taj Mahal for the first time, go to a party, meet new people.* Staring out the window, she looked forward to catching up with her friend Kalpana. *After all, she mused, it had been a year since they had last seen each other.* It would also be the first time she would meet Kalpana's husband, Satish.

Paris dozed off until they stopped for a few minutes to pick up more passengers. As the train reached full speed again, she wondered about passion and why it was so destructive, so powerful and yet so tangible and then unattainable when it got out of control. *Why is it so addictive and so possessive when its power is unleashed?* She thought about her friend Kalpana and her husband, the perfect couple, in love and together. They were a couple who had made a commitment. A couple who had bonded in marriage based on their love for each other. *Did they keep secrets from each other,* she wondered. The steam train whistled intermittently and stopped often, taking on huge loads of passengers. Some squeezed into the train and sat on the floor. Others found space on the roof and dangerously hung on until it was time to literally jump off. A group of orange-robed disciples entered the compartment and sprawled with agility on the floor, where they opened tiffin boxes and ate lunch.

Sometime later, the man in white next to her, began reading from Tagore's "The Crescent Moon". He read aloud the poem, "The First Jasmines" and this caught Paris's attention. She turned to him and remarked "what a lovely poem". For the rest of the journey they discussed poetry. With Agra approaching, she began to feel at home.

As the train pulled into Agra, she spotted with mounting excitement, the first dramatic glimpses of the faraway Taj Mahal which appeared to be floating on a bed of clouds. For the first time since leaving Alex she felt elated. It was the same wonderful sensation she would feel bathing her toes in the glacial waters of the Himalayas.

Paris's hotel car was waiting for her outside the station. The narrow streets winding in and out of the main throughway were crawling with people, intermingled with mooing cows, and a flock of hysterical hens. Stray dogs lay listlessly on the eroded roads as vehicles whisked past them at lightning speed. Meanwhile a shabby, barefooted rickshaw wallah, collected a young couple who had travelled on the same train. He picked them up by the platform and carried them with sprightly, nimble feet through the tiny alleys against the insanely honking traffic.

Jovi's speedy arrival at The Cascades in Agra was made possible when he arranged for his luggage to follow him later. Jovi heard the monotone pleas of a rickshaw wallah soliciting business. On the platform, he had carefully shielded his companion from the din and mayhem by putting his arm around her shoulders. They pulled away from the station within seconds, avoiding the main route leading to The Cascades. Exhausted, his companion retreated to her room. Jovi stayed behind to attend to business and await the arrival of Paris, who still had not checked in.

The grand gates of The Cascades opened onto manicured, green velvet lawns. Cascading fountains shot into the air at any given moment in shades of pale blues and mauves. Paris had seen rare sights like this before when the sun rose behind the mountains creating a rainbow effect across the undulating valleys. As she approached the hotel entrance, she could not help but raise her gaze to the magical view of the Taj Mahal in the distance.

The main hallway leading to the lobby was dotted with tall pillars carved with snow-white leopards and their young. Miniature fountains cascaded between them in perfect harmony. Glimpsing garden terraces filled with pink anemones, Paris began to long for home. A young girl with tawny eyes and copper-coloured hair greeted her. Wearing a yellow and red sari, she wreathed Paris with a chain of fragrant white jasmine blooms. She placed her hands together and bowed.

"*Nameste*, Miss Cassidis. Welcome to Agra, our land of passion."

In the lobby where refreshments were being served, Jovi waited in suspense. Had his prediction been correct? He had to know! He had to find out if she was the one. Could she be the woman he had always held close to his heart? The woman he had dreamed about as the years eluded him? The woman who resembled the painting hanging in his home? With burning anticipation, he waited for her to appear.

As Paris came through the main hallway, his heart throbbed wildly and his legs weakened. Trying to get up without falling over, he held onto the arm of the chair and pushed himself upright. Jovi's legs swayed as he felt his energy falter at the knees. A flood of tenderness ran through him, and then passion. He walked toward her, taking in her slim, statuesque frame. Paris was elegantly turned out in a lavender suit, holding a large camera bag. The garland of white jasmine blooms around her long slender neck excited him.

"You must be Paris Cassidis, the famous CMS photographer?" his deep self-assured voice lingered in the air.

She swung around. "That's me," Paris said, caught off guard.

"I've seen your pictures and admire your artistry," Jovi said breathlessly. "Thanks!" she replied, feeling embarrassed, feeling waves of desire. She bit her lip and hoped he wouldn't notice her attraction to him.

"Is this your first time in Agra?" he inquired, genuinely interested.

"Well, yes it is," Paris said, starting to feel an inexplicable impulse to touch him.

Jovi's towering stature took her by surprise. His beige and cream linen shirt was intricately embroidered with fine gold thread at the cuffs and collar. Paris noticed his red leather shoes coiled in gold at the tips. Observing his broad shoulders and muscular body, she thought he must be an enthusiastic sportsman. His thick black hair curled about his forehead, making him look irresistibly charming. However, it was his eyes which captivated her. They were full of meaning, deeply engaging. She noticed them change colour from blues to greens, as if his emotions defined the colour of his eyes. Paris felt short of breath. Her emotions overwhelmed her, and she felt as if she were melting.

"Have you set your eyes on the Taj yet? The Cascades has the best view in town," Jovi said unable to move away from her.

"Yes, once from the train and again just now. The pictures don't do it justice. This is my first time here and I can't wait to visit the Taj Mahal, but I'm not on assignment!" Paris explained cordially, trying to ignore his probing looks.

"The times to visit are at sunrise and naturally, at sunset. The gates close at 7.00 p.m. If you're the last to leave, the caretakers will let you stay on to take pictures until they go home" he said.

"Thanks, I'll try to make it at sunrise tomorrow. I've just arrived and need to get organized." Paris regretted saying that and wondered if she should go now instead and invite him along.

"Don't forget to visit the Red Fort built by Akbar before the days of the Taj," Jovi said, longing to hold her, as the seconds ticked by.

"Yes of course, I've read about it. I believe it's pretty impressive, almost two miles long." *That's it, she thought, I'm definitely going to ask him to show me around.*

"Yes, and there's a marble pearl mosque inside. It's impressive!" he added, powerless to let go.

"I've read about the fabulous peacock throne," Paris ventured.

"Oh … er … that sadly was lost … many years ago," he replied, realizing she was extremely well read.

"I'd like to visit the glass palace at the fort where the walls are inlaid with tiny mirrors!" she continued.

"You'll enjoy that. It's the best example of glass mosaic in the country." *That's it,* Jovi thought, *tomorrow I'm going to the Taj too!*

"Is it? Thanks for the tip. I'm very excited!" She exclaimed, wondering whether she was more excited about Jovi or the Taj.

"Well, I mustn't keep you any longer, you must be tired. It was a pleasure to meet you and I do hope you enjoy your trip." Jovi fought the impulse to kiss her. The subtle fragrance of jasmine lingered in the air as he struggled to walk away.

"Thanks." Paris regretted he was leaving so soon. Pointing to her garland as if she were helpless, she called out. "Oh … er … would you mind … it's pretty heavy."

"Certainly … with pleasure!" Lifting her garland, he swept her hair aside, lightly brushing her cheek. She could not help but notice his long fingers, his elegance.

"There you are," Jovi said, unable to draw himself away.

"Thanks!" Paris wondered whether his eyes were blue or green.

"Well … enjoy your trip," he said, grinning with pleasure as if he had already won her heart. Holding the garland in one hand, Jovi turned and left.

As Paris moved to the front desk, the large hotel was bustling with activity. Groups of people checked in and out. Porters fumbled with bags while polished well-mannered receptionists dealt with jet-lagged, irritable guests. In no time at all Paris had checked in and received her room keys. A porter escorted her to the Mirabai suite.

"Surely this must be a mistake?"

"No, Madam." the porter insisted. "This is the room. I'll check with reception if you wish."

"I didn't reserve a suite! It's a mistake! Thanks anyway, I'll call them."

Paris tipped the porter and called reception.

"Good evening Miss Cassidis. How may I be of service?"

"I believe there's an error. I booked a single room with a view but not a suite. It must be a mistake."

"Let me check, Madam. Please hold the line", replied a receptionist. She waited patiently on hold.

"Miss Cassidis, I've checked your reservation and there is no mistake. The Mirabai Suite has been booked for you with the compliments of the management and we do hope you'll enjoy your stay with us," the receptionist confirmed.

"Who's responsible?" Paris asked, wondering what was going on.

"The management, Madam. If there's anything else we can do to make your stay more comfortable, please don't hesitate to call us."

Perplexed by the management's generosity, Paris unpacked nonetheless. Her mind was not at rest. Images of the attractive man she had met in the lobby kept coming came back to her. She craved to see him again. Her thoughts then drifted to Sutton since he had known about her trip to Agra and the hotel she would be staying in, but she then ruled him out. It was not his style and he rarely meddled in the affairs of others. Alex, however, had been deliberately kept in the dark, so she ruled him out too. Kalpana, she concluded, must have arranged this.

In Europe, Kalpana had been her backbone, a solid rock to lean on when times were tough. She had lifted Paris's spirits during dramatic escapades in the war zone areas of Africa. Her wit and vitality were sorely missed in CMS. She had also been Paris's link to India, and with her friend's subsequent resignation, Paris had lost the physical presence of an honest and witty friend.

Their time together in Srinagar when they had launched the radical newsletter Sidelines, had been more than memorable and had ultimately tempted Paris to ask Kalpana to work with her in CMS. With little persuasion, Kalpana had agreed and they had spent twelve exciting, but gruelling months together in Liberia and Sierra Leone. Kalpana had opted to go home after one year, homesick for Satish, her fiancé, who lived in Agra.

The balcony of Paris's suite, tastefully decorated with Italian terracotta tiles, looked onto the magical vista of the Taj Mahal. A small cascading waterfall to one side of this balcony was rimmed with a rampant collection of colourful anemones. The large divided petals opened as a gust of wind blew past. Water from the fountain sprayed her as their honeyed fragrance reminded her of her childhood, walking hand in hand with her father in the valleys. Paris plucked a couple of them and placed them in a vase next to her bed.

At dusk she began to take pictures capturing the incredible sunset in Agra. The view of the Taj Mahal again overwhelmed her senses. The many shades of the dome began to change before her eyes. Paris thought that the Taj was living a hundred battles, a thousand dreams, a multitude of memories and emotions. To her, it never gave up as it sat idly and majestically alone, noble and daunting, grand and radiant, dazzling with beauty, sparkling with rubies, perched in sublime elegance on its imposing throne.

Early the next morning Paris left with a picnic basket and her cameras. Wearing a lavender sari bordered with white tassels, her long black hair, sleeked back, revealed her oval face and her almond-shaped eyes. Her hair looked like black silk thread falling to her waist.

As she approached the imperial gates leading to the looming mausoleum, Paris began to take pictures, deftly changing cameras and lenses. The formal gardens and water canals leading to the domed white marble structure were flanked by cypress trees. The pool and their fountains reflected the dome of the Taj Mahal.

Finding a solitary corner overlooking The Red Fort, she sat down against a cool marble pillar and listened to the strains of an Islamic hymn worshiper. A swarm of bees flew past followed by a yellow butterfly, which flitted near her cameras.

"May I join you?" Towering over her was the same striking man who had greeted her at The Cascades. His white linen jacket slung over his shoulders, he propped his body against the pillar and removed his sunglasses to examine her, and be examined, more directly. As the blood rushed to her head and the sun blinded her eyes, Paris saw his handsome profile, crinkled her nose and willingly moved over.

"Oh yes, come and join me," she said smiling shyly, as her heart raced out of control. "Have you visited yet?" He inched closer. He put his dark glasses away and rolled up his sleeves, revealing a large gold bracelet with the letters JOVI. He pulled up one knee and rested his arm on it. They sat shoulder to shoulder, their knees occasionally brushing against each other.

"Well, actually yes and no. There's so much to see, so much to digest that, once I've seen it all, I know I'll want to go back and see it all over again. I don't think I'll be able to tear myself away tonight." Paris enjoyed confessing her complete immersion to this exciting man. Jovi knew what she was feeling.

"I feel it every time I see the Taj," he murmured, "and every day it looks different from the day before. The locals believe that the Taj comes alive with dancers when the village sleeps. That's really when the entertainment starts."

"You know, I can see it all now. I believe it," she said, as she studied his strong hands. Paris couldn't help noticing that on his left hand, he wore a large square diamond ring set in white gold.

He continued, "Shah Jahan made Agra the capital of his Mughal Empire and for fifteen years, twenty thousand workers were employed to create a masterpiece of Mughal architecture."

"I didn't know that," she admitted. *I wonder if he's married.* "It must have been a horrendous job, particularly in this heat. Where did they find white marble?" she inquired.

"Makrana, 200 miles from Agra. The same white marble is still quarried there today."

"How did they get it here?"

"I believe that huge slabs of marble were hauled by cart one piece at a time. Would you like to visit the tomb? It's cooler down there and I'll show you the remains of the royal lovers!" He grinned.

Oh, that famous grin of yesterday, Paris thought, returning the same affectionate smile. He got up and gave her his hand, which she accepted as a trade-off for losing his shoulder. They walked together to the dimly lit tomb.

"Shah Jahan completed the Taj in 1649. He'd originally planned another tomb for himself. A black marble replica across the river, to link to the white one, but his dream never came true."

"Why, what happened? Did he die before he could do it?" Paris really knew the story, but wanted to hear him tell it.

"No, I'm afraid the story is a sad one, are you sure you want to hear it?"

"Yes, of course, I'm absolutely fascinated," she said, looking closely into his eyes. *They are blue and green* she thought, *oh no, they're blue, oh but now they're green!*

"Shah Jahan spent the last seven years of his life imprisoned by his power-hungry son in The Red Fort. The tower looks onto the Taj and so he spent his days gazing at the monument he'd conceived for his great love."

"When did he die, at what age?" Paris asked wondering how old he was.

"No-one knows the exact dates, but some believe he died at the ripe old age of seventy-four."

They continued to walk around the tomb. Jovi took Paris's hand and guided her as she sprinkled red rose petals on the tombs. From then on, he did not let go of her hand until dusk.

They spent the rest of the day talking. Their intellectual abilities meshed, and he was as impressed with her relaxed sense of humour as she was with his. Paris liked his refined manner and the way he talked about history, politics, his work, his career, his passion for horses and sports. Her natural instinct to be on guard when getting to know someone now disappeared as she found herself talking freely about her life with CMS and her friends in Switzerland. Jovi was particularly interested in her role as a humanitarian worker with aid agencies, when she was not shooting for CMS, and they spoke at length about the refugee children who were close to her heart.

After discovering that they both had connections in Switzerland, they were able to discuss cafes, restaurants, cinemas and ski resorts they both knew well. Jovi, a keen skier, talked about his love for the sport and she admitted the fun she'd had snow-boarding. Daylight passed into dusk and Paris, noticing she'd had little time to photograph the changing moods of the Taj, decided to shoot a couple of rolls before leaving.

"I'd like to take some more pictures," Paris said, "and I've probably taken up too much of your time. Are you staying at The Cascades? Can I take you back later? I have a driver," she offered.

"Thanks but no - I have errands to run and a dinner engagement." *Should I ask her out a drink later?*

"You still haven't told me your name," she said, hoping it would be something romantic like the letters on his bracelet.

"Jovi."

"That's nice."

"Thanks, it's been a pleasure," Jovi said gently, wondering whether he should ask her to join him for dinner.

"I hope I'll see you soon?" she replied, disappointed at the thought of Jovi leaving her without making another rendezvous.

"I'm sure we will, very soon. Have a good evening, Paris," he said kissing her on the cheek and finally letting go of her hand. Regretting not having asked her out for the evening, Jovi then decided that he had indeed been wise to be cautious. He was, however not accustomed to vacillation, especially about women.

The full moon began to rise. Paris slipped into a trance and began to dream about what this effigy of love, the Taj Mahal must have meant to its creator, the Emperor Shah Jahan. He had given birth to the memory of his love, in the form of a marble monument, to protect and shelter the tomb of his dead wife so that their love would last forever. *This is the only building in the world a man has ever built out of passion for his woman*, she mused. Mumtaz Mahal, his devoted queen, his trusting wife and the mother of their fourteen children, died in childbirth, leaving the emperor desperately lonely for her love.

Paris stayed late to shoot the breathtaking images of the Taj changing its profusion of diverse facades. She began to take pictures of the caretakers before they left for the day too. On arriving back at The Cascades exhausted from the heat of the day, she barely noticed the colourful fountains and ignored the fireworks display.

The lobby was alive with gossip, tea drinkers and cocktail parties. Children played hide and seek while their parents looked on indulgently. The elderly read the papers and the young teenagers scouted for potential infatuation. Ignoring it all, she went directly to her room.

The midnight blue skies appeared as if they were drowning in a pool of brilliant stars. A thousand constellations engulfed the Taj Mahal. A wedding feast in full swing on the lawns below her balcony caught her attention. Slipping into the shower Paris washed her hair quickly, wrapped a towel around her body, in bare feet and dripping wet hair she walked out onto the balcony to see the first moments of the couple's married bliss.

Reflecting on her day with Jovi, she felt alive and full of vitality. Paris also experienced an unusual sense of relief -- as if something good was going to happen. That special something that could last forever had been with her that day at the Taj Mahal. It was a special moment involving love, which had won her heart. Jovi's pride as well as his refined personality and gentle manner had mesmerized her, but his eyes had taken her beyond passion, beyond anything she had ever dreamed.

However, marriage and its significance weighed heavily on her mind. As Paris watched the glamorous, superficial revelry, she felt India had cheated itself. Love and sadness overwhelmed her. Peering down at the party and then seeing in the distance the colonies of makeshift huts, the poverty-stricken communities made her feel compassion for those not so fortunate as she. Paris sat down at the writing table and began to compose:

> *India imprisons me*
> *Like a hand at my throat*
> *I'm jammed against the wall*
> *Poverty and peace*
> *Just another wedding*
> *Just another feast*
>
> *Fiery sunsets every night*
> *Yet another wondrous sight*
> *Grandiose glory, don't miss the treat*
> *Hellish beauty and the blinding heat*
>
> *A painful reminder of days' events*
> *Bundled together in huts and tents*
> *Splendid sunsets in contrasting hell*
> *A never-ending story that no one can tell*

Paris put down her pen and returned to the balcony. She caught sight of Jovi dressed in a pale gold suit. He was circulating among the wedding guests. He was engrossed in conversation with a mixed crowd -- young and old, married and unmarried, and mostly financially well off. Jovi glanced up to the Mirabai suite several times before spotting Paris on the balcony wrapped in a white towel, drying her wet hair. Their eyes met and held until Jovi was distracted by a flock of young ladies.

Her heart was pounding. Paris knew she was falling in love again. Filled with desire for Jovi, she sought refuge in sleep. And then she began to yearn again for Alex, a love, a memory still so alive that she was unable to put it to rest. As she slept, thirst woke her several times, as dreams haunted her. Then images of Alex's naked body lying close on her bed trapped her. The moments she had spent running her fingers through his thick, blond hair, kissing his lips just days before, now felt a lifetime ago. Paris asked herself, how she could fall in love again so soon.

The door opened letting in the yellow glow from the dimly lit corridor. Paris jolted awake and gasped when she saw Alex standing alone, his naked silhouette glowing in the dark. She tried to speak but no words came to her. Alex walked over to her bed and put his finger to his lips. He held her in his arms and kissed her on the back of her neck. Releasing his grip, he pulled away the lace straps of her flimsy negligee. Paris watched as he removed it and tossed it onto the floor. The silky material floated away naturally. There was something different about him. She swallowed, desperately trying to find her voice. Unable to utter a word, Paris looked on uneasily, unable to move her hand to touch him. Alex's right hand moved down across her stomach. The tips of his fingers moved to the top of her bikini line. She moaned. Alex slid down by the bed so that his knees rested on the floor. Paris could feel her body heat rising. She could hear his heavy breathing. Alex had left the door slightly ajar.

The door opened and Jovi entered. He looked taller than she remembered him. His nude body, she saw, was strikingly sexy, the curves around his crotch beautifully sculpted. The top half of her body rose momentarily off the bed. Paris arched her back, her long black hair spilling around her naked form. Her rounded breasts, firm and heavy, reverberated in unison with the beat of her heart. There was no sound now except for her own laboured breathing. Jovi was smiling. Alex retreated and stepped aside into the shadows. He looked on. Paris noticed Jovi's eyes. How erotic she thought. Jovi draped his arm around her waist and pulled her closer, roughly at first and then he took one nipple into his mouth and flicked it with his tongue. Rapturous with delight she gasped with pleasure. She struggled to keep her eyes open. She noticed the yellow light from underneath the door, then it disappeared just as quickly. Paris was alone with Jovi. His body was warm. His scent wildly intoxicating, the smell of fresh jasmine blooms. They were face to face. She reached up and brushed a curl from his forehead. Jovi's aura enchanted her. She strained to reach his mouth. Seconds later he burrowed his tongue, devouring her lips. Locked in paradise she moved with excitement, tossing her head back and forth, the muscles of her thighs contracting, her hips dancing with pleasure. Frantic, ecstatic, pleading for more, Paris clutched him around the shoulders digging her nails into his flesh. Jovi mounted her, pinning her arms back against the dishevelled sheets. Letting her loose, he traced the line of her body from her fingertips to her waist with both hands. She surrendered willingly, desperately, urgently, hooking her legs over his hips, gripping onto his lean and hard frame. Exploding with pleasure, Paris felt an intensity she had never known and he finally slid into her warm moist innocence, frantically satisfying her uncontrollable desires, bringing her up and beyond her wildest dreams.

Waking up Paris opened her eyes. She reached over and snapped on the light. The door was locked, bolted from the inside. Her negligee lay crumpled on the floor beside her bed. She pulled the ivory satin sheets over her head and slept.

6

Golden Organza

$\mathcal{I}$t was at the Palace of Malamar, years ago, that a curious and significant royal wedding took place. The princely groom arrived on horseback in dignified splendour. The royal champion carried the prince under the arches leading to the gardens where he met his bride. The white stallion's leather saddle was painted gold. The horse trotted ceremoniously; composed and elegant. Dismounting close to the lavishly decorated ivory wedding canopy, the prince took his place opposite his bride.

The priest began to chant while the guests sang and danced under the arches. Young girls giggled among themselves as they witnessed the marriage of the royal heirs of their small kingdom. Children played hide-and-seek in the safety of the vast palace grounds. Women bantering with the men gossiped endlessly. Loose-limbed waiters, in starched Nehru suits, scurried with perspiring palms as they served the guests cold drinks. Skinny children pulled at their turban sashes and threatened to dislodge them for fun.

The bride, dressed in red silk and carrying a golden organza shawl, wearing a large gold nose ring decorated with filigreed flowers, held her head down. Her raven hair had been smoothed back with oils, her hands and feet hennaed with patterns of rose petals, a symbol of this auspicious occasion. The cries of joy from married women alarmed her, so she reached for her mother's comforting hand. The four posts holding the canopy in place were decorated with white curtains flowing in perfect synchronization. Pots ablaze with red trumpet blooms were shattered by a strong gust of wind and were strewn across the slippery white marble.

The classical melodies made the bride feel sleepy. Sitting so long without respite, the bride asked her mother's permission to sleep. Feeling sympathetic, she held her daughter's hand and rubbed her back with the other.

The priest raised a white cotton screen between the couple while he chanted holy verses. To bless the couple, he showered them both with rice and rose petals, calling upon the stars and the planets to bestow them with happiness. The bride woke up. The groom offered her a ceremonial sweet called laddoo. She did not raise her head but waited for him to bring it to her mouth. The bride and groom then crossed their arms one over the other and held hands. The bride's twenty-one bangles in red and white ivory caught the light as she moved, their gentle jangling almost musical. Then the couple touched each other on the head but their eyes did not meet during the whole ceremony. This bonded them to the force of life. The cloth was removed and presented to the bride's mother.

The golden organza shawl and the groom's red cotton scarf were tied together while the priest lit a small open fire inviting Agni, The God of Fire, to witness and bless their union. Purified butter, oats and sesame seeds were spooned onto the fire as an offering to the gods.

The groom rose and walked around the fire with his bride. The sacred stones, placed at the four corners of the fire, which they touched with their toes, represented religion, prosperity, responsibility and salvation. The mother blessed the couple, placing a red spot, a tikka, on their foreheads. As she sprinkled them with rice, a young girl, newly wed, whispered into the bride's ear, "May you be married forever."

The two legendary thrones of gold, once belonging to King Trikuta, sat majestically in the courtyard waiting for their new heirs. The upholstered fabric, woven with pure gold thread, celebrated Malamar's heritage. This emblem of royal pedigree was embroidered with lions to commemorate the great lions of Gir.

The royal couple took their places on the thrones. The bride tugged at her mother's sari and insisted on leaving.

"No, not now my love, not just yet, my darling."

The bride slept as the wind grew stronger and knocked over another pot of red trumpet blooms, smashing it to bits.

7

Jewels and Jealousy

$\mathcal{U}$nable to get out of bed, Kalpana Salwani reached, like a near-fossilized dinosaur, for a bottle of scotch. It slipped out of her weary fingers and rolled onto a priceless Oriental rug. Glue-eyed and jelly-legged, she lurched forward in the bed. Slouching over the side, she grabbed the bottle and poured. Her head rolled back and reality melted back into her veins.

Last night her marriage had disintegrated. Love with Satish had blossomed, bloomed and withered. In vain, Kalpana had tried to draw him closer, tending to all his needs as a devoted wife and lover. Arrogantly self-possessed, Satish took pleasure in turning a blind eye, and marriage had inevitably driven them apart.

Recollecting the arguments of the previous night, Kalpana realized that her romance had ended a long time ago. She repeatedly asked herself how she had failed. Had she made the sacrifices expected in a marriage? She had given him her love. She had comforted him and sympathized with him. Becoming his confidante, his friend, had all been to no avail?

Kalpana swallowed again quickly. Her washed-out, sickly appearance heightened as she let the daylight filter in. This followed a race to the toilet where she vomited. Wearing an ungainly cotton nightgown, she slumped onto the white tiles. Satish was not going to give in easily. His harsh treatment had driven her to drink and laid her wide

81

open to his vindictive taunts. In a grim turn of events, his poison revealed his passion for mockery.

When did the drinking start, Kalpana taunted herself, searching for an answer. She had never depended on anything before, let alone alcohol. Once it had served as a pleasurable pastime, never a compelling need. Her pride had been her independence and self-control – her firm grip on reality. It had been these fine qualities which Satish had been attracted to. He wanted his woman to be self-assured, strong, even bold, so why had he driven her to drink? When had they stopped making love? Why had he left their bed?

Removing her nightgown, Kalpana looked at herself in horror. She had become fat. She had put on so much weight. Had she eaten to compensate for the lack of love, a love she could not get from her husband? To eat was to be happy and now she had destroyed a well-toned, youthful body. How could she be attractive to any man, like this?

Brooding between gulps of water, Kalpana convinced herself that she wasn't ready to face the truth. Deep in contemplation, she dressed hurriedly. She longed to begin again, erase the errors of the past and regain the strong will that had driven so much of her existence.

Nevertheless, even anticipating his venom, Kalpana prepared to meet with her closest friend. Avoiding the mirror, she poured another shot. It was the shot that would give her enough confidence to get through this day. She deeply regretted her distorted appearance and damaged sex appeal.

So much had happened since Kalpana had last seen Paris. Returning to India to marry the man of her choice had enhanced Kalpana's then-thrilling love affair, but eventually it had destroyed her self-respect. In a country where arranged marriages were still the norm, falling in love was a rebellious pastime reserved only for the wealthy. Satish was suave and overtly sexual. Kalpana was petite and charming and he was her magnetic, dark-eyed beau. This tall handsome man had finally lured her into his bed. Kalpana had become obsessed. Her obsession consumed her and gripped her heart to the point where Kalpana was unable to see through Satish's web of lies and compulsive infidelities.

Bewitched, Kalpana had decided to leave CMS to pursue him. In truth, Satish had escalated their romance with letters filled with endearments and passion. These letters convinced her to return home and soothe his aching heart. His letters had cast a magic spell and obscured her vision. Satish sought sexual conquest; Kalpana dreamed of enduring love.

Elegant, cynical and world-weary, Satish Salwani preyed on women. They were his weakness. Intelligent ones amused him. Superficial beauties only redoubled his sexual desire. Wives, on the other hand, he tempted with sadistic novelties. The chase fascinated him and he enjoyed breaking tender hearts. On one occasion, Satish showed up on the wedding night of an old girlfriend and coaxed her into adultery. He was the devil in shining armour, just as on his own wedding night he doomed Kalpana when he told her he did not love her after all.

By going to Europe and joining CMS, Kalpana had made a long-lasting impression on Satish's family. Her social position within her close-knit community was immediately elevated to the status of "honourable lady of intellectual mind". These liberal thoughts bonded the two families as it guaranteed she would eventually bear an offspring of the same calibre. Since both families were wealthy, Kalpana had finally met her financial match.

At the outset, Satish too had been more than impressed. While Kalpana was in Europe, he talked endlessly about her, boasting about her glamour and intellectual prowess. The quest became dangerously exciting when he first met her in Srinigar after a business trip. When she told him she was leaving for Europe, he thought he was falling in love with her. More importantly, however, Kalpana had innocently divulged that she would inherit her father's estate. For Satish this information served to intensify the hunt.

However, when success in CMS later catapulted Kalpana into elite society, this generated a bitter rivalry between them. Her journalistic achievements only amplified his failures, Satish took pride in belittling her. Pushing her aside had been his means of retaliation, his ammunition to ostracize her.

Not long after their wedding, Satish had dutifully obliged his aging father by assuming the family business, which quickly inflated his brash public persona. The lucrative business of quarrying granite and marble from Makrana not only kept Satish on his feet, but now conveniently distracted him from his miserable personal life.

Prisoner of her own heart, Kalpana envied her friend Paris and her love for Alex. *How perfect Paris is*, she thought, coating her face with makeup to hide the dark patches of sleepless nights. Paris could love with such ease and honesty. Kalpana ached to be like her friend.

Paris waited for her friend alongside the pink anemones, sipping sweetened lemon juice on the terrace near the lobby of her hotel. Feeling relaxed for the first time since leaving

Alex, she drifted off, dreaming about Jovi. The morning sun filled the terrace with rays of light and she sat there undisturbed, bathing in the warmth of the day. Kalpana spotted her from a distance. Muffled in baggy blue jeans and a large white T-shirt and clutching a pair of expensive sunglasses, she walked unsteadily toward her friend. Disturbed by a loud inarticulate cry, Paris opened her eyes. At first she did not recognize Kalpana with her short coffee-coloured bob and rough voice. The soft-spoken, slim woman she remembered, had disappeared. Then Paris jumped to her feet.

"Kalpana, I've missed you so much, CMS hasn't been the same without you and neither have I for that matter!" They hugged affectionately.

"Paris, my darling, I've missed you too. Just look at you in that colour, *yaar*! You're more glamorous than ever. You've still got that sparkle in your eyes," Kalpana said, noticing Paris hadn't changed a bit. Her short skirt and jacket were the latest fashion. Paris, she noticed, was wearing a single strand of pearls with matching earrings.

As Paris tried to come to terms with her friend's transformation from petite to bloated, sadness washed over her. Kalpana wriggled uncomfortably. Her plump fingers twisted around her sunglasses and a trickle of perspiration fell onto her ample breast. Paris ordered another lemon drink.

"Oh … I'll take a scotch, if you don't mind, *yaar*? I've had a busy morning and a stiff drink will do me good!" Fidgeting again with her sunglasses, she decided to put them on.

"Tell me about CMS. What's been happening since West Africa? I still think about the days we were together … you, me, Alex! Wish I'd had the courage to stay on, *yaar*. I get my monthly copy of *Cyber* to keep me informed! The photos are incredible, how do you do it?"

Paris reached tenderly for her hand.

"Hey, when you left … everything changed. We lost our lucky mascot! Kalpana, you were the lightning streak, the most engaging spirit we've ever known. You were born with the gift of laughter and a sense that the world is mad! Everything changed when you left!"

These words pleased and relaxed Kalpana. The two friends laughed together reminiscing, dwelling on moments spent together. As the morning passed, Kalpana managed to regain some elements of her vibrant personality. Removing her sunglasses, she inadvertently exposed the dark circles and puffiness under her eyes. Distracted by a screaming toddler, she hunted for a cigarette.

"And Sutton, how's he doing?" she asked, lighting up.

"He fights the good fight … sometimes he wins and sometimes he loses … but … you know what he's like. He'll slit his throat before he'll retire. He's got his eye on Alex, thinks he'll be able to take over when the time's right."

"And Alex, what does he think?"

"It's hard to tell, he's a field man. I can't quite picture him behind a desk!"

"Why isn't he here with you, *yaar*?"

Suddenly Paris, a non-smoker, wanted a cigarette. Here she was, she thought, trying to forget him and now having to explain. She felt worse than ever about leaving Alex without saying goodbye, but still decided to spill the facts.

"Well … I've left him! And I've … resigned and I'm going back to Kashmir for good!" she said calmly, wishing Kalpana hadn't asked.

"Oh Paris, I'm so sorry … you didn't say … going back … resigning … leaving … Alex … going to Kashmir? It's not safe!"

"I know, I'd hoped you'd come with me, for old times' sake?"

Kalpana felt the vigorous warmth of friendship overtake the mounting levels of alcohol. She listened with gratitude and tried to cast her mind back to the last time anyone had wanted to be her friend.

Paris reflected, "Remember the saying, "fools rush in where angels fear to tread"? Well … right now I feel like a fool. But, I've got to go! I've been in worse situations. I'm under no illusions, it was dangerous when we were churning out the newsletter and it's worse now. Will you come?" Paris implored, hoping her friend would say yes and pack her bags right away.

"I can't. Satish will never let me!" Kalpana said, ashamed.

"Why?" Paris asked, knowing the answer already but wanting to hear it straight from her friend.

"He's crazy, turned into a mean beast and won't let go of me. I'm afraid I'm stuck here for a while."

"What's going on?" Paris demanded, feeling animosity towards her friend's husband.

"Long story, but I've tried everything to save my marriage. Still these are difficult times for me, besides my health …" she stopped, took a deep breath, put on her sunglasses and stubbed out her cigarette. Kalpana reached for the scotch.

"Enough about Satish. Tell me about Alex, why did you two split up?" she inquired, trying to change the subject. Putting down the glass, Kalpana lit up again.

"I've left him because *he* left *me* no choice!" Paris said, unconvincingly. "Explanation, please. I'm not buying that!" Kalpana said flatly, wondering why her friend was being unusually vague and evasive.

"I had to leave! Alex made no commitment and neither did I. But I did protect myself by not giving him my soul … and he respected me by not asking for it," she said, even more vaguely.

"Could you stop flitting around and tell me straight? What did he do?"

"He broke my heart!" Paris confessed, feeling better for it.

"How?"

"He couldn't say *I love you*!" she admitted, releasing the pent-up tension, the things that had been on her mind for so many months.

Kalpana was shocked to hear this. She had always expected Paris to do something wild and unexpected but she had felt sure she would settle down with Alex and that the two of them would somehow organize their schedules and make their love work.

"Alex, full of ego and ambition … guess he hasn't changed?" Kalpana muttered under her breath, adding, "Suppose he's off to Baghdad?"

"That's right, he goes anywhere Sutton sends him even though it means risking his life, and that's not the kind of life I want! I can't be with a guy who never refuses an assignment. I want a home and a family, but more importantly, right now I need to figure out who I am!"

"But why come home now, you're still young and you've a lot more working years ahead of you. I still think you could have worked it out with Alex, somehow, somewhere."

"I left because I felt it was right for both of us. I loved him too much. I was willing to give myself to him but he still couldn't break away from his own demons, his own inhibitions, his own feelings, call it what you want … his love which he has refused to share with me."

Kalpana, disillusioned with love, wondered with abject fascination how emotion could be as sharp as a blade and as soft as the feathers of a dove all at once. Her expectations for her friend had been grand. Love for Paris, she believed, was inevitable. It was a road she believed Paris would eventually go down, surviving admirably despite its trials and tribulations.

"So, my darling Kalpana, will you come with me to Kashmir?" Paris asked again, crossing her fingers.

"Even if I wanted to, I couldn't get further than Jammu!" she said, sadly. She would have done anything for Paris but this was a bad time. Even opening her eyes hurt like hell.

"Why?" Paris asked, disappointed and reluctant to make the trip alone.

"When are you leaving?"

"Day after tomorrow, hopefully, depending on flights. They're often cancelled at the last minute."

"The place is heavily guarded. You must have a press pass. I don't have one. Flying into Jammu is the least of your problems! It'll be trickier at checkpoints! How did you plan to get home?"

"Sutton's given me a CMS ID card and I've press privileges. In theory, it should be a breeze. As long as you stay with me there shouldn't be a problem."

"Paris, I can't come with you, *yaar*. If I do get detained they won't let me go lightly ... sorry but this time you're on your own!"

"Wait a minute, what *is* the story with you and Satish?" Paris asked realizing that Kalpana was avoiding the subject. "I sense you're hiding something from me!"

"It's bad, what can I tell you? What do you want to know? I fell in love and he fell out of love. Life is not as romantic as you think!" Kalpana said, cynically. "I never see my husband. I have no professional life and I spend my time going from one women's luncheon to another. I'm bored, Paris, and when I think of our time together in Europe I want to cry."

"You can still come back. Sutton Pearce needs to replace me and you would be the perfect candidate!"

"What, divorce Satish and run away to Europe? Come on Paris, you must be joking *yaar*! You've been in Europe too long! Anyway, I wanted to come back to India, to be close to my family ... you know they moved away from Kashmir to the capital. My heart is here. There I'm a foreigner, it's not my home. I've always wanted to marry and settle down. I was terribly in love. I wanted to marry before I joined CMS but my parents convinced me to wait. After I met Satish I missed him terribly! I was dying to get to Agra ... the city of romance," Kalpana said sarcastically and then continued completely out of breath.

"When I got back he'd changed. At first, I thought I'd changed ... and then he introduced me to whisky! My life since then has been hell! It's in ruins! There's no way out! I wish I could leave him, but I'm too weak, I've no courage! We spend our time arguing. Oh Paris, why do you think he's not here with me now? Satish doesn't love me! I'm old and fat and he can't bear to look at me." Kalpana stubbed out the cigarette and snapped her fingers rudely, ordering another drink. This time round she ordered a large orange juice, freshly squeezed. Letting go of all inhibitions, Kalpana sobbed, attracting glares of disapproval.

"I'm sorry, please don't cry. Dry your eyes and tell me what you've planned for us today?" Paris asked light-heartedly, hoping Kalpana would be able to drive.

Kalpana, pulling herself together, reached for her mirror and fixed her face.

"With the party crowd you can never tell," she mumbled as she wiped away greyish grains of smudged makeup. "Before the party, at the Abbey, there's a polocross tournament later this afternoon. If you've never seen polocross, we should get there before teatime."

"Lead the way!" Paris said, relieved that her friend had bounced back.

"Go and get your party clothes. Meet me outside, I have my new Land Cruiser, so let's get out of here!"

The Abbey, a hotel built above the foothills of Agra was once the summer palace of a bygone Maharaja. It hosted a monthly polocross tournament between the Knights and the Tigers. Lying abandoned for many years, the lodge had been lovingly resurrected by the British as an exclusive country club. The grounds, sprawling over acres of green velvet lawns and blooming apple orchards, were filling with enthusiastic onlookers.

The forests were an ideal habitat for deer, tigers, bears and many other animals. The Abbey, where rain falls abundantly, is a fashionable play station for prosperous executives and their families. Its unhurried atmosphere, cool breezes, misty mornings and endless tea parties caught the attention of the landed gentry years ago, who then began to cultivate tea on their rambling estates. It was their love for polocross which boosted business at the hotel which now attracted large, enthusiastic sporting crowds. It was also the place to be seen and a venue where love matches could blossom and wither. Rooms were reserved, sometimes at an hourly rate, to accommodate a whim or the infamous *polo sex*. Polo sex participants were determined by who won what on tournament day.

Satish, arrogantly attractive, confidently pulled up in a new metallic silver Mercedes convertible. Wearing a black leather jacket and fitted black leather pants, he removed his Versace belt and threw it into the back of his open-top car. He was in a good mood. An additional new purchase, an irresistible white stallion, had aroused him. Satish was in love with his horse and it showed. Swaggering towards the stables, he stopped momentarily when he noticed Jovi in the far distance walking alongside a beautiful beast. He sneered and headed straight for White Shadow who was nibbling from the palm of his stable boy's hand. Dismissing the lad, Satish began to caress the horse's thick greyish-white mane. The horse's elegant comportment made him whisper silly love sonnets into his ear. Whipping off his black leather jacket, roughly tossing it aside, he undid his fly. Satish mounted the horse, then with deliberate rhythmic motion swayed from side to side, caressing its mane, brushing his thighs against the fine soft hairs of the animal. He sat upright, arched his spine, threw his head back and slipped the fingers of his right hand into his open fly. His body quivered. His fingers danced around his crotch in mounting excitement. Stroking himself, easing his hand back and forth, he grunted with pleasure. Satish was breathing heavily now, urgently squeezing harder, more desperately this time. Closing his eyes in sheer ecstasy, he began to thrust himself into his wet moist hand clutching onto the horse's saddle with the other. Satish moaned louder. His breath was hot, his mouth dry as he increased the speed, sweating at the temples, seesawing back and forth, heightening the pleasure, pumping quickly, deeper and faster until his body jerked and shuddered and it was finally over. His body collapsed limply on the back of his horse. Satish lay alone locked away in his own release. He dismounted, zipped up his fly, grabbed his jacket and walked away, utterly satisfied, and ready to win.

Jovi walked alongside his favourite horse, Bashful Beauty. Carrying his helmet in one hand and guiding his shiny black mare with the other, he patted her luxuriant black flowing mane with paternalistic attention. Her long tail swished elegantly as they spent the afternoon together.

Bashful Beauty, a fine-boned, elegant mare, by far the most exquisite horse in the tournament, stood at Jovi's side. Her dignified poise and noble bearing gave her the coveted nickname "The Polocross Princess". The crowd had come to see Bashful Beauty, the beauty of all beasts, a legend with a rare winning streak. Her speed and stamina were undeniably superior to any other horse Jovi had owned. Her appetite for racing was insatiable. She not only had the swiftness of a cheetah and the intelligence of a fox, her relationship with her master, as everyone could see, was astonishing. When Jovi spoke, she would respond, when he walked, she would obediently trot beside him in perfect symmetry, awaiting her next instruction. Bashful Beauty was Jovi's favourite horse.

The tournament was close to ending when Paris and Kalpana arrived. They made their way to the crowded stadium, where a small crowd had gathered to cheer on the last players. Paris recognized Jovi mounting a remarkable looking horse ready to play in the final round. There were cheers and a standing ovation as he approached the pitch. Music blared out of an enormous loudspeaker playing "We Are The Champions." A large video screen showed a close-up of Jovi on his gleaming black mare. Thunderous applause greeted him as the crowd stood up and sat down in waves. Jovi then regrouped with the rest of his team. He was labelled No.1 for the Knights, opposite his opponent, Satish, who played No.1 for the Tigers.

Paris and Kalpana settled down to watch. In the centre of the field, Jovi lined up in front. Satish stood opposite. The other players positioned themselves at the rear. The umpire threw the ball, and the players galloped to score. Satish scored the first goal, alarming the Knights. White Shadow showed off his splendid agility by carrying his rider close enough to the goal post to ease in the ball. Satish rode on in delight, lifting his racket in the air as the crowd rose and cheered him. As he entered the next round the tables turned and his winning streak faltered. This time round the Knights scored, draining the blood from Satish's face, making him sweat profusely at the temples. He grunted angrily, kicked his horse with his stirrups and yanked its reins so hard that White Shadow yelped in pain, and pan-icked. The horse bolted and bucked, throwing Satish out of the saddle and onto the muddy pitch. The match was halted while a first-aid team examined Satish. They tried convinc-ing him to get on the stretcher, but he refused and stormed off. Infuriated by his failure to win the match, he bumped into the nurse as he stomped off the pitch.

The Knights strutted around the stadium in good humour, holding their rackets high in the air as victors of the day. The music still blared out into the semi-circular stadium. With Satish gone in disgrace, the Tigers dispersed soon after. Jovi dismounted Bashful Beauty, removed his helmet and stroked his horse affectionately, while feeding her carrots. Then, after shaking hands with the stable boy, he patted Bashful Beauty on the back and reluctantly released the horse to him.

Jovi walked over to a young woman and embraced her. Paris, who had been following his every move, studying his every expression, stood there open-mouthed in utter disbelief. Her heart missed a beat and she began to feel light-headed. Her knees gave way and she lost her balance, gripping onto Kalpana's arm to steady herself. She noticed that the young woman who was holding his hand never let it go for a moment. Paris's mind began to spin. *Had he a wife, a mistress, a toy woman to play with when he had nothing better to do?* She agonized. *What kind of man was he really?* Paris began to doubt him as well as her own feelings. Two years of loving Alex had not only shattered her faith in love but had made her doubt her own ability to choose a suitor for herself. And now to suffer again, in this way, with a man like Jovi who outwardly seemed open and honest. Paris turned pale, her skin resembling porcelain. She clenched her fists. To avoid embarrassing questions from Kalpana, knowing how inquisitive she was, Paris tried to hide her disappointment. *She had only spent the day with Jovi*, she told herself; *that alone was not a true sign of a lifetime of love.*

The young woman was of medium height and very slim. She wore a short blue and white polka dot dress and a large white hat. This was ruffled with blue and white polka-dot bows and a thin net covering her eyes. Her white suede shoes, most inappropriate for the muddy surroundings, Paris thought, looked enchanting but terribly out of place. Nevertheless, she was a woman attractive enough to draw attention.

"Paris, you look like you've seen a ghost. What's wrong?" Kalpana asked.

"I'm fine," she said, unconvincingly. She did not want to talk about Jovi just yet. She felt unprepared. Besides, Alex was still on her mind and even though she had discussed her emotions with Kalpana, she had felt deeply hurt when Alex refused to confess his love to her, just days ago. This feeling of commitment now seemed diminished by uncertainty. Chiding herself for jumping to conclusions, she eyed Jovi and the young woman as they talked.

"I'd like to rest before dinner and change. Is there anywhere I can go in the hotel?" Paris sounded tired and on edge. She began to feel that jet lag was finally catching up with her. And she needed to be alone.

"Yes, we've a suite here … you can go there to change. But I was hoping you'd stay at my place tonight *yaar*. It's not far from here … 45 minutes or so."

"That's very kind," Paris said, wondering where Jovi was staying the night.

"Let's go into The Abbey. I'll show you around. You can meet Satish later. Oh … by the way … he was the guy over there!" Kalpana said pointing to Satish.

"Oh right … I see … over there … who's the number one rider?" Paris inquired, matter-of-factly.

Kalpana nodded towards Jovi.

"You mean *him* over there … oh Paris I must introduce you to him." Lowering her voice to a whisper, she raised her eyebrows and said, "He's the man in every woman's dreams." To make matters worse she continued, "He's the man no woman can get close to."

"Except for that young lady with him now?" asked Paris irritably.

"Which woman … oh her … I don't know who she is … I've never seen her before. He's never been here with anyone. He comes alone and leaves. No one knows much about him. He's pretty mysterious, you know!"

Satish swaggered over, gin-soaked and smirking.

"Aren't you going to introduce me, dear?" he inquired as he fixed his eyes on Paris. *Another womanizer*, Paris thought, and pitied Kalpana for not having tuned in to this before.

"I'm Paris … Paris Cassidis. I'm sure Kalpana's mentioned me before," she said shaking hands. Satish held on even as she tried to pry her hand away.

"Well, yes," he said, "in fact … I must know more about you … than you know yourself!" He suppressed a laugh and she sensed his compelling need to be as flirtatious as possible.

"My wife never told me how beautiful you are," Satish continued. "It's a pleasure to meet you. I've been following your work with *Cyber*. Kalpana makes sure I'm regularly updated," he added, sarcastically.

Kalpana addressed her husband directly. "Did you enjoy the match, *dear*?"

"It's a curious thing! People only ask if you are enjoying yourself when you aren't!" Satish said, poking fun while trying to come to terms with his own defeat. Kalpana was pleased with herself. With Satish successfully defeated by the dashing Jovi, his bravado would dwindle for the rest of the day. Realizing that today was her lucky day, Kalpana began to enjoy the sight of Satish sulking. *Maybe I do have a chance to put my life together and start again*, she thought. *Maybe I can be like Paris. Live with the same serenity, the same inner peace that she does.*

"Have you congratulated Jovi, *dear*?" Satish inquired as he shook her out of her reverie. "He played like a prince. We should congratulate him," he proposed, trying to elevate himself in Paris's presence.

Paris, not keen on the idea, changed the subject.

"You've a beautiful stallion! What's he called?"

"Ah, I see you've got good taste, my dear, and an eye for sublime beauty. His name's White Shadow. It's only his first tournament. I'm upset he lost this time, but next time he'll win! Let's go and congratulate Jovi?" Satish proposed again.

"I don't think that'll be necessary," Paris replied, "look … he's on his way over!"

Jovi crossed the lawns alone.

"Great stud, Satish, he's a winner!" Jovi said admiringly. "How's the knee?"

"Oh … I've had worse … it's nothing!" Satish winced, deliberately.

Greeting Kalpana with a hug, Jovi told her how nice it was to see her again. Kalpana, enjoying the spectacle of her husband's humiliation, hailed a light-footed waiter in a white tunic. Jovi, turning to Paris, grinned affectionately, catching her off guard as his eyes changed colour from blue to green and then blue. A surge of desire overcame her, she could barely speak. Satish introduced them, but oddly enough neither referred at all to their previous meetings. Paris observed the woman in the stadium. Jovi, noticing, offered no explanation.

"Shall I see you tonight at the dance?" Jovi asked Paris softly, as he looked into her almond-shaped eyes fringed with dark lashes.

"Yes, I certainly hope so," Paris said as she imagined dancing with him.

"Well … until tonight then. Hope you'll grant me the first dance, Miss Cassidis."

"I'd love to," she said, overwhelmed by his persona, his penetrating gaze. She couldn't resist him nor could she utter the words echoing in her mind. *Who is she, Jovi? Who is she?*

Paris took a few moments to sit on the bed and think about what she wanted. Alex had disappointed her by not declaring his love and now here was a man who was using his charm to entice her into his lair. *Entice*, she thought it an interesting word. After all, one can only be *enticed* if one is already enchanted. Enchantment could lead to love and she felt torn between the two. Jovi was becoming an addiction. Was she overreacting, or just seeking an escape from her sorrow? Yet she could not get him out of her mind.

Paris carefully opened the gold box and removed the extraordinary necklace. Holding it up to the mirror she unfastened the gold pin and put it around her neck. The red ruby necklace dripping with a multitude of sparkling diamonds formed a V-shape dangling from the neckline to her voluptuous cleavage. For the first time in many years, Paris began to accept its significance.

Removing the necklace, Paris dressed in silk walked onto the balcony overlooking the lush green forests. She heard the wind howling and watched the blossoms twirl around in the air like snow in spring. She sat staring into the horizon but saw nothing but emptiness. Paris was deep in thought. She was hurt.

Paris stroked her body from her neck to her breasts around her hard protruding nipples to her stomach and then between her thighs reaching down to her toes. Just to please him, just to feel him, just to sense him, just to seduce him.

Paris dressed for the party. Everything had to be perfect. She asked herself many times if he would appreciate her ruby red dress, her hair swished up, pinned with diamonds, the colour of her lips and the polish on her nails to match.

Paris adored Jovi, but she knew she could not have him. She knew. But still she took the trouble to draw pleasure from thinking about every minute detail, so not to disappoint him. Paris returned to the balcony with sadness in her heart. Tears ran through her but none showed. She wanted to feel the twirling blossoms against her skin. She wanted to feel close to him.

And yet he had come to The Abbey with another woman. Paris started to tremble. She feared he could never be hers. She sat with agony in her heart. With jealousy soaring within her.

Paris prepared to leave her room. Tying to convince herself she really did not mind the other, she knew this was a lie. Paris put her agonizing thoughts aside, to the back of her mind. She told herself that she was special to him and that gave her courage and made her feel safe. This easily soothed her doubts.

After much deliberation she finally decided to wear the ruby necklace. She wanted to excite him. She wanted to be irresistible to him. But no matter how hard she tried she could not help feeling hurt. Paris was so afraid of losing his love. She was so afraid. Paris braced herself for the evening and stepped out of the suite.

Soon after, alone, holding the gold wrought iron banister, whilst proceeding carefully down the staircase to the melody of "Rhapsody in Blue," Paris attracted every onlooker's attention. At the sight of her off-the-shoulder evening gown, Jovi thought: *ravishing*. He inhaled sharply, unprepared for her breathtaking beauty, her incredible presence. The chiffon scarf floated about her as she walked, her hips swaying slightly. She momentarily touched her hair. *Perfection,* he thought.

The crowded dance floor was already in full swing. Guests were now doing a fiery version of the Charleston to the updated tunes of "Maple Leaf Rag" followed by an old-time favourite, "The Original Rag Tune." Small groups of dancers performed with a band called The Jazz Swing. As Paris entered, she could not help but notice the magnificent ballroom, dripping with a unique collection of Venetian crystal chandeliers. Underfoot a luxuriously thick cherry-red wool carpet stretched the length of the floor. Rosewood tables were decorated with white orchids. Kalpana, turned out in a flattering, full-length celery-green evening gown. She spotted her friend and went over to say a slurred hello, holding yet another glass of scotch. Fascinated by Paris's jewels, she was interrupted before she could ask about them.

"Kalpana, I've never seen you drink so much!" Paris scolded her over the pulsating beat.

"That's The Abbey for you," Kalpana slurred out aloud over the din. "It helps pass the time … and you … what are you drinking?"

"I'll stick to cool white wine. It's going to be a long evening, I can see that. Who are all these people? They're great dancers … what a band! And the music is wonderful. I feel like dancing …"

"Oh … look … there's Jovi. He's alone … wonder what happened to the young woman he was with this afternoon … I'm surprised he didn't go back to Agra. After all, it must be a devilish job running a hotel like The Cascades!"

"I had no idea he was the manager … well that explains it then," Paris yelled over the commotion.

"That explains what?" Kalpana called out as the loud music changed into a frenzied tempo.

"Why I've been checked into the Princess Mirabai Suite when I only reserved a single room." She hollered into Kalpana's ear.

"You're ... not making sense again, what ... do ... you ... mean?" Kalpana demanded. They moved over to a quieter spot.

"Well, when I arrived at The Cascades, I bumped into Jovi and we started talking. The next thing I know I had been mysteriously booked into the most exclusive suite in the hotel with no explanation and *at no charge*! What do you think of that? I thought *you* had something to do with it!" Paris said, sipping her wine and wondering where Jovi had disappeared to.

"Are you sure you don't know him?" Kalpana asked, impressed, and slightly envious.

"Of course not ... I've never seen him before nor have I had anything to do with him. But every time I see him ... every time I talk to him ... I feel ... as if I've known him all my life!" Paris's eyes flitted around looking for Jovi while she nibbled on the edge of her glass.

Kalpana cooled the end of her nose with hers. She squinted, about to release valuable information.

"What's the matter?" Paris said, "Now you're the one who looks like you've seen a ghost!"

"Jovi's not the manager of the hotel!" she revealed over the pandemonium.

"Well ... who is he then?" Paris inquired as a waiter whirled by, tripped, and toppled a tray of champagne glasses.

"He's not only the illustrious billionaire owner of Dream Machines, which I'm sure you've heard about in your travels, but he also designed The Cascades and owns it. Satish's family supplied the marble from the quarries in Makrana. Rumour has it that Jovi built the hotel in memory of a woman he loved, but no one knows the full story! He arrived in Agra a few years ago. Although he's very wealthy … he's very … discreet! He doesn't throw his money around, particularly on women, that's for sure!"

Kalpana hesitated and giggled before she babbled on. Paris looked at Kalpana's empty glass of scotch and hoped it was her last.

"You see all those lovely ladies around him?" she said pointing with her glass.

"Yes," Paris replied.

"They're all young and unmarried. None of them will be able to catch a man like him, though, but they're sure trying … just look at them. Bewitching … beautiful … maybe … but … dragons in the dark! He can see through them all. He knows what he wants and it's not them!"

In the hubbub, Kalpana signalled the waiter and ordered another scotch. Mesmerized by Paris's necklace, she asked about it.

"Where did you get this? I've never seen anything so unusual. It's just beautiful and so overwhelming!"

"Oh … er … it's a family heirloom." Paris mumbled, distracted by Jovi as their eyes suddenly met. Aroused by his penetrating gaze, she felt hypnotized, weakened.

"It's sensational … where'd you get it … you're brave to wear it … it must be worth a fortune!" Kalpana said, unable to take her eyes off the necklace.

Trying hard to hide her feelings, Paris found herself telling Kalpana about Jovi.

"Kalpana, I think I've fallen for him!"

"Who?" she replied, baffled.

"Jovi … Just like all the other women … I feel an idiot … I'm going to leave tomorrow! I won't be able to stay at the hotel knowing that I'm crazy about him! I'll leave for Jammu tomorrow, and it's just as well," she said flatly, as the panicked waiter returned to clean up the broken glasses.

"It looks like he's on his way over!" Kalpana cried out with excitement.

"Look," Paris said, "when the dance is over I'm going back to Agra. Sorry darling, but I won't be staying at your place tonight! There's a flight I can catch …"

Smiling, Jovi came up to Paris. His eyes, she noticed, were a delicate shade of aquamarine tonight.

Jovi offered her his hand asking, "Would you like to dance?"

Oh that husky heart-stopping voice, she thought. Paris held out her trembling hand, as she had at the Taj Mahal. She entered the world of Jovi, a world where she knew she belonged, a world of magic. Unable to refuse or utter a single word, Paris took his hand and entered the weightless world of passion, the rapturous world of love.

"Look, Jovi, when the dance is over, I'm leaving … I can't see you again."

"I'll never let you go!" he responded confidently.

"I've missed you, Jovi," she murmured, to her surprise. He held her in his arms and led her to the dance floor to the final, gentle chords of Frank Sinatra's "Something Stupid."

"I've been thinking about you too," Jovi replied as the rhythm suddenly changed into yet another hot swing. As the first chords of a samba belted onto the floor he swayed her back and forth seductively.

"I'm not sure about this … I hardly know you," Paris said breathlessly as he tried to kiss her.

"Let me kiss you softly, like the gentle ripples of a stream, and that way you'll get to know me a little bit better," Jovi teased her as his arm stayed firmly fixed around her waist. Their lips then touched as they glided around the dance floor.

"But Jovi, how can I be sure of your … love?" she implored.

"Let me show you," he told her in a seductive voice, leading her swiftly to a dark corner away from prying eyes. There, he pressed softly against her. A dark curl tumbled over his eyes and she ran her fingers through his hair to remove it. He smiled warmly as he traced her slim silhouette down to her waist. Hugging her hips against his, he moved his hands to the small of her back, stroking her to relax her. Paris, desperate for him to take complete control, lay in his arms. She leaned back against the wall and closed her eyes, imagining Jovi's lips on hers again. Jovi, sure of her innocence, relaxed his hold and inched away, driving her delirious. Determined, she pulled him back. Paris opened her eyes to record the moment. Brushing his body against her gown, lightly at first for some time, he began to pull her closer, caressing her perfect curves. Paris parted her lips invitingly and they kissed, dizzy in love.

The music ended and the master of ceremonies made an announcement.

"At midnight we celebrate the Festival of Colours. For those of you who do not wish to be sprayed, you had best leave now. Those of you who do, stay and enjoy. The night is still young!"

"What going on?" Paris asked, as the drum beat pounded out a tango.

"It's time to leave, come on, let's go!" Jovi announced, leading her briskly through the ballroom.

The master of ceremonies started the countdown.

"Ten, nine …"

"Hurry up, my darling, or we'll get sprayed!"

"Seven, six …"

"With what?" she yelled over the noise as he dragged her out of the ballroom.

"Five, four …"

"With colour!"

"Three, two …"

"What colour …?" she insisted, her heart throbbing with excitement.

"Powder … coloured powder. It's the holy Festival of Colours!" he exclaimed, out of breath, whisking her into the library at top speed, locking the door behind them.

"One! Burst the pockets! Let the powder flow!" commanded the master of ceremonies.

A huge fire crackled in the library which was romantically lit with hundreds of candles shaped as lotus flowers, floating in bowls of coloured water. "Goodness", Paris gasped, "this is unbelievably romantic … you knew?"

"Of course, and so did everyone else. This is the *Holi* party held annually at The Abbey. Didn't Kalpana tell you?" he said, locking the door. Sweeping her off her feet, he carried her to the sofa.

"No, not a word!" she said drawing a deep breath. Wrapping her arms around his neck and nibbling on his ear, Paris lay close to Jovi, listening to the riveting tunes of the tango. He caressed her tenderly, touched her lips lovingly, while she ran her fingers through his thick black hair.

Intrigued by her unconventional necklace, he asked her about it.

"This is the most extraordinary piece of jewellery I've ever seen. Is it from your family?"

"Yes it is, why do you ask? It's the first time I've worn it. I feel quite daring."

"I'm glad you did! It's magnificent! I would say this one is priceless … am I right?"

Oh those eyes again, Paris thought, before replying.

"Yes, it's a family heirloom."

"Next time don't bedazzle me!" Jovi said teasingly. He slowly slid her dress below her breasts revealing a strapless bra. His strong searching hands aroused her even more, leaving her gasping with excitement, twisting and turning in his arms. His body, hard and inviting, almost crushed hers. He took a deep breath and removed her bra.

She quizzed him, "Jovi, how can I be sure of you?"

"You have to trust me, my love. But you can feel how I feel about you, can't you?" he said as he withdrew his mouth from hers.

"Yes I can, my lover," she whispered in his ear.

"Tell me, my darling, are you still a virgin?"

Paris sat up abruptly, rearranging her dress indignantly.

"How dare you ask?" she protested, retrieving her bra. "How terribly presumptuous and, undignified!"

"Don't be angry with me. I have to ask you, my dearest."

"Why? What difference would it make? Would you love me less if I was not?"

"I'd love you just the same!" Jovi said, trying desperately not to hurt her.

"Then … what if I asked *you* the same question? What would you say? How much are you willing to reveal?" she challenged.

"If you ask me … I'll tell you," he said calmly, as if this moment was inevitable.

"Well?" she inquired, raising her eyebrows.

"Paris, I've never slept with a woman I didn't love completely, and I'd never let a woman near me unless she felt the same way about me. If I am the first man or the last man in your life, then it still has to be right."

She grabbed him so roughly he nearly toppled over.

"Say those words again, Jovi," she whispered imploringly and then she told him what he wanted to hear, she told him the truth. This admission thrilled him, and unable to resist, Jovi began to kiss her even more passionately than before, his mouth warm, loving, and intently seeking. And she responded with equal passion, letting him into her heart. Lying in his arms, she felt elated as he hardened against her. She kissed him excitedly, more intimately this time, as she parted her lips at last to let in his insistent tongue again. And then he began to caress her tongue with his own, languorously, until she sobbed with tears of joy.

"Why are you crying?" Jovi asked, as he wiped away the tears.

"Because this is how I imagined it to be. This is how I wanted to fall in love. Here with you in this room ablaze with floating candles. I'm so happy Jovi, please make sure this works forever. I want you so much."

He tempted her with sonnets, with lines from love songs, with poetry, lingering over every phrase as he enchanted her.

"I don't have to touch you to feel you, it is the mystery of the chemistry of love," he whispered softly in her ear. *"I don't have to dream to imagine, a perfect alignment of passion, it is the magic of the mystery before love."*

The stimulation was so thorough, she could hardly breathe. He persisted, unable to conceal his feelings, desperate to declare his love.

He continued whispering. *"I don't have to romance you to love you, it is the mystery of the chemistry of time."*

He watched her gasp as she hung onto every word, knowing she could hardly breathe. Paris became the painting he once saw and couldn't quite place, his lover, his fantasy, his wildest dream. Paris knew she could not let him go.

The library glowed faintly while the music died down. As they lay in each other's arms the fire sizzled and the candles gradually flickered out. Jovi's words of magic meant he could not break away from the intimacy they had created. He was unable to let her go. He removed the diamond hairpins, her hair tumbling down while he repeatedly lavished kisses between her breasts.

"You sway my passion, you move my mind," he groaned, *"I cannot stop loving you."*

Jovi's hair glinted in the moonlight. He stood up, removed his waistcoat and tie, unfastening the buttons of his shirt.

She removed his shirt and massaged his upper back, tracing his form down to his trim waist. The music faded from the ballroom. All was silent except for the sound of their breathing. She closed her eyes and slid her hand under his belt feeling his excitement, his delirious passion. Her body ached and she moaned almost screaming with desire.

Kalpana hunted for her husband. She had grown hoarse as more people dropped by to say hello. Standing at the bar, she finally spotted him flirting openly with a girl in a short black dress, black fishnet stockings and a red leather belt studded with gold bolts. The dress was cut low enough for Satish to spend most of his time looking into it, she noticed, and the woman was skinny enough to slip into his trouser pocket. Her mousy, hennaed hair, excessive black eyeliner and frosted green eye shadow, infuriated Kalpana. On each ear, the girl wore two large round gold earrings. As Satish backed her up against the wall while whispering into her ear, he moved in on her, hands pressed to the wall above her, his chest rubbing against hers.

As she went over to drag him away, Kalpana tried to stay calm.

"Satish, let's go. I've reserved a table."

"Go? Go with you? You must be joking. You go and enjoy yourself. Eat with your friend Paris," he replied, raising a mocking brow. Satish half turned toward her, keeping one arm very near the girl in black.

"You should be with me!" Kalpana exploded.

"I'm staying here … don't tell me what to do!" Satish fired back.

Hurt and desperate for a drink, she went back to the bar only to see her husband now in a passionate embrace. Nauseated, Kalpana began to heave. She let go of the scotch, splashing it onto the carpet, and sprinted to the restroom where she vomited, then passed out on a couch.

Kalpana awoke shortly before dawn. Making out the first hints of light she quickly washed her face and rearranged her hair. Her green glittering dress looked woefully sad as she inspected herself in the restroom mirror. Eager for a change of clothes, she hurried to the suite. On her way up, gripping the banister, she recollected the events leading up to her blackout in the toilet. Satish's behaviour had not only disgusted her, it had broken her spirit. With stoic determination, she decided that this was the final straw. She would tell him to go to hell and give her a divorce. Feeling better for the decision, she thought about Paris and Jovi, who she had noticed were living in a world of their own. This was the enviable world of new love and first moments. As she saw them dancing, she had suddenly craved the same kind of love.

The door to the suite was ajar. Peeking inside to find no one around, Kalpana went directly to her bedroom. As she opened the unlocked door, to her horror she saw Satish standing half-naked. His shirt hung off his elbows, his black trousers were wrapped around his ankles and his hands firmly gripped the skinny shoulders of the young woman Kalpana had seen him with earlier. The girl was kneeling on the floor, her face inches from his rock hard and ready groin. It was at this moment, she would reflect later, that her world disintegrated. But it was also the point in her life when she found courage so profound, so intense, that it catapulted her into believing in herself and in her own separate world. Satish hadn't noticed Kalpana. He hadn't heard her gasp in disgust. Desperately Kalpana tried to find a sound or the words to attack him with. She felt empty.

Disturbed momentarily by the whiff of her familiar scent, Satish slowly turned to look at her. Their gaze locked, his in sadistic mockery. Her presence only excited Satish. He smiled at her wickedly, tauntingly. Challenging Kalpana, hurting her with his arrogance until she could bear it no longer, he then ignored her gaze. Grabbing the kneeling girl harshly by the shoulders he pumped into her mouth, swaying her back and forth, groaning and grunting with ecstasy. Satish quivered in delight, arching his head back as she noisily devoured him. He was unable to contain the pleasure of his jerking body. Sick with humiliation, unable to find the strength to move away from the door, Kalpana watched as he reached his climax, as the sweat poured from his temples and the release was complete. He finally brushed the girl away, and she edged out the room seemingly unruffled by Kalpana's entrance.

He knew he did not have an explanation. "Kalpana, let me explain … it meant nothing!"

And she knew that he had finally killed their love, as had been his intention. But she also knew that no matter how hard he tried he would never be able to break her. Kalpana, grabbing her coat, ran from the room a different woman.

Jovi was dressing Paris.

"No … not like that my darling … you'd better let me do it," she whispered as he helped her put on her bra, lavishing breathless kisses on her breasts and upward along her neck.

"Here, let me help you then … you shouldn't have to do any of this," he protested.

"Here … look … I'm fine … over here … just … just grab it where my fingers are … right …!"

He brushed back her long hair which now fell radiantly around her shoulders.

"Sorry about your hair, the chignon was lovely!" he said, straightening her necklace.

"Thanks, I did that just for you."

"Aha … what else are you going to do … *just for me*?" he said teasingly.

"You're gorgeous!" she uttered lovingly.

"No, you're gorgeous!" he whispered back.

"Oh, no, Jovi you're gorgeous," she said firmly, and they laughed together, then their lips touched softly and neither of them could pull away.

Kalpana put on her coat while pounding down the staircase, screaming blasphemy. Pursued by Satish, who had buttoned up his trousers, he was screaming back at her desperately trying to put his shirt on.

"Why won't you let me explain, Kalpana?"

A small crowd lingered, intrigued, they watched the spectacle.

"Don't touch me, you bastard, get away from me. Go back to your slut, you piece of shit!" she spat back.

Satish, taking the keys out of his pocket, replied haughtily, "I'm driving you home. You're drunk, woman!"

Snatching the keys, she snapped, "Not anymore, you little shit!"

Jovi replaced the necklace around Paris's neck. He took her hand and led her out of the library. Kalpana, now buttoning up her coat came rushing down the stairs.

Her face streaked with tears, she caught Paris emerging from the library and clutched onto her arm.

"Paris," she pleaded, "come with me tonight. I can't be alone with Satish, not tonight, please."

"What's going on … what's the matter … you're too distraught and in no condition to drive … what did he do?"

"Please, let's just get out of here" Kalpana pleaded, heading for the exit.

Jovi turned to Paris.

"Paris, don't go, try to stop her if you can."

"Oh God, this isn't turning out the way it should, I'll do my best", Paris groaned as she hurried after Kalpana. Taking off his black jacket, Jovi ran after Paris and draped it over her bare shoulders. He ran to get his car so he could follow them.

Satish stood at the Mercedes. He reached for his leather belt lying in the back seat and angrily snapped it in the air. Paris followed Kalpana who was now in the courtyard striding defiantly to the car. Kalpana took the driver's seat and

Satish, scornfully, reluctantly sat beside her slamming the door hard, hurtling the belt into the back. Paris managed to dodge it as she climbed in. Kalpana shot out of The Abbey at full speed and then stopped abruptly outside its gates. It was the moment before dawn was about to break. Grey and pink rain clouds opened the skies.

"Get out, Satish!" Kalpana roared.

"Drive the car you crazy woman!" he spat back.

"You son of a bitch," she convulsed as she darted down the road again. "You knew I would come in. You left the door open deliberately. You bastard ... You filthy bastard!"

"Don't be a fool, the girl doesn't mean anything to me ... slow down ... give me the wheel ... stop the car ... let me drive ... or you'll kill us all!"

"I want a divorce! I hate you," she said, letting go of the steering wheel with one hand and slapping him across the face. Taken by surprise, Satish said nothing. In frenzy Kalpana began to cast a spell:

"God of the forces of chaos and of hostile desert lands, destroy this clone, this monstrous serpent-headed bastard man!"

Paris listened, wondering how Kalpana could recite the description of Sutekh, the Egyptian god of chaos so masterfully. Time to get out, she thought. Holding onto the edge of her seat, Paris wondered whether getting out was going to be an option. She clicked in her seat belt instead. Kalpana replaced her hand on the wheel and the car sped dangerously along, screeching around several hairpin bends. Stunned, Paris was speechless. As they approached the tip of the mountain road leading to the tea estates the Salwani family owned, Paris noticed with deepening concern how close to the edge of a steep precipice Kalpana was driving. Suddenly Kalpana was no longer even driving on the road. Hoping that her friend would let her get out, Paris looked behind for other cars and finally spotted a Land Cruiser. In another fit of anger, Kalpana took one hand off the steering wheel again and began to yank at Satish's hair. Then she used both hands to thump him on the head. To Paris's surprise, Satish offered no defence, no resistance. He let his wife pound him. Kalpana violently regained control of the vehicle, instinctively realizing how dangerous the situation had become. Paris feared for her life. She could not reason with Kalpana because her friend seemed too angry and completely devastated. Paris decided there was nothing she could do or say to make the situation better.

A few hair-raising minutes later, Kalpana swung the car carelessly to the edge of an overhanging mass of hardened mud, deliberately swerving along the cornice. To Paris's relief, Kalpana finally looked into her rear view mirror and spotted the Land Cruiser in hot pursuit. She stopped abruptly, the car now perched precariously on the mountain precipice with a rear wheel hanging over the side.

"Paris, get out," she ordered "Please! Go! Just get out of the car!"

Paris did not move. Cemented to the seat and shaking with shock, she was unable to reach for the door.

"Paris, get out!" she instructed more softly. "Jovi's behind us. He's come for you … look, we'll be in touch soon … go! My so-called husband and I should do this alone."

Paris felt she was letting her friend down, but obligingly got out.

"Be careful, Kalpana. Please," she urged, wondering whether this might be the last time she would see her.

Soon after the Mercedes slowly edged back onto the road. Standing alone on the cliff, enveloped in Jovi's warm black jacket over her evening gown, Paris shivered. The Salwanis tore down the mountainside. She watched them disappear into the horizon. The breeze blew her hair about her face and she slipped her arms into Jovi's jacket, pulling up the collar. The Land Cruiser drove up.

"Hop in, Paris," said Jovi reaching out for her. Shivering, she got into the car. He put his arm around her shoulders and cuddled her.

"Are you warm enough now?" he inquired.

"Yes Jovi … I'm getting there … thanks … I just can't believe this has happened," she said, with sadness.

Then he started the engine and headed back slowly.

"It was bound to happen. Satish has been asking for trouble and now he's got it. They've been like this since I've known them!"

"Well … that doesn't help … does it?" Paris said, instantly regretting the comment. "Why did they marry … why? Why does he make her suffer?" she added.

"This isn't the first time it's happened … but it's the first time she's caught him in the act … with his pants down! Come on … forget it … it'll be all over in the morning."

Feeling chilly, she said. "Jovi, can you take me back to The Abbey? I need to get into something more … comfortable."

"Come home with me?" he said lightly, as if he were throwing a bag of tricks into the air. Stunned, she looked over her shoulder while he concentrated on the road.

"Where's home? You still haven't told me a whole lot about yourself!" she replied, leaning over and kissing him on the neck.

"Well, for one, it's close to where you live!"

"Oh really … and where's that?" she inquired curiously.

"Say you'll come with me and you'll never look back!" Jovi replied mysteriously.

"I can't!"

"Why?"

"For one thing I have to get back home, and though I'm crazy about you I can't suddenly let go of everything and just move in!" *Is he completely sincere?* she wondered, running her eyes down his thighs and remembering how lovingly she had caressed them just a few hours ago.

Jovi's inexplicable insistence puzzled her. *Does he want me that badly?* Yes, they were both in love and yes, they had spent the night in each other's arms, but it didn't make sense. Was he counting on her refusal? Was he guarding a secret? *Was it something to do with the woman in the stadium?* she mused, for he had not mentioned her at all. *Was that it?* He had not mentioned his family or his childhood, even after she had divulged most of her past - with the exception of Alex and one other detail. Jovi continued to mystify her.

"Where are you going?" Jovi asked her as they drove up to The Abbey.

"Sambara, close to Jammu in Kashmir."

He stopped outside The Abbey. He reached over and opened her door. Before letting her out he said, "That's not telling me a whole lot!"

119

"It's a long story … I'm not sure I want to go into it now!"

"Passion cannot be taken … it waits to be accepted. Paris, come with me now and never look back." She turned to look into his eyes, searching them for confirmation that he really did love her.

They had stopped at The Abbey for barely half an hour. The lobby was deserted. The worn-out waiters had long since gone home leaving the band to clear up their own mess. After showering quickly, Paris headed for the library. Jovi caught sight of her as she went in.

Just hours ago they had been in each other's arms and now they were barely talking. The fire had died out. Cinders occasionally sputtered onto the marble floor. Inside that very room she could still smell and taste him. Slumping onto the sofa Paris closed her eyes and dreamed of Jovi. He stood by the door and watched her, once more the object of his erotic imagination.

Later that afternoon at The Cascades, a distinguished-looking man in a beige suit left the private elevator by the terrace where Paris was sipping tea. She was concealed behind a wall of flowers. Recognizing Jovi, Paris melted. Perhaps this was the time to tell him her dark, innermost secrets, she thought. The night before, in his arms and then in his car, she had considered telling him about Alex, instead of saying nothing. With this in mind, she half-rose, trying to attract his attention. But he walked past her, stopping a few feet away from her, intent on another woman waiting for him.

When the young mysterious woman Paris had seen at the stadium put her arms around Jovi, Paris froze, lowering herself back in her seat. The woman's white chiffon scarf floated off her head and onto her slight shoulders as she moved to grip Jovi's hand. Paris, speechless, observed that she was not only very pretty but terribly attached to Jovi who had been hers less than twenty-four hours ago. He was the friend she was to confide bittersweet secrets to. He was the partner she had chosen for her lifetime. He was the lover of her dreams, the perfect representation of honesty and trust - and he was throwing it away as Satish had done with Kalpana. *Is there no justice, no truth, no honesty and no dignity left in this poor world?* she asked herself. As love and respect disintegrated, she overheard their conversation.

"Jovi … I'm so sorry … you know how much I love you," the young woman sobbed.

"Don't be silly, you know I'll never leave you! You're all I have … we'll always be together. We have to hurry … it'll take us an hour to reach the airport in this traffic."

Recognizing the unusual fragrances of the night before, Jovi looked around for Paris. Paris watched from inside the terrace. Then, he walked away, through the lobby and into a waiting taxi. Paris stood up.

"Prove me wrong, Jovi", she muttered, as the knife so brutally stabbing her in the heart penetrated even further.

The breeze rushed in, petals of white jasmine swirled in the air like snowflakes in spring. The balmy days of April filled the lobby with sensual fragrances. Fallen red petals swirled at her feet. A yellow butterfly fluttered onto her hand and flew off. Too betrayed to have faith in anyone or anything anymore, Paris went to her room and wept.

Paris prepared to leave The Cascades. The doorbell rang and she opened it, half expecting to see Jovi there with an apology. It was the bellhop holding a silver tray with an envelope on it. She inspected it eagerly, hoping it was a letter of explanation from Jovi. Ripping it open, she found a fax from Sutton.

"Deepest sympathy ... I know how much you loved your father. Sincere condolences from all your colleagues in CMS. Sutton Pearce." Grief-stricken, Paris began to tremble.

8

Stars and Himalayan Nights

The timely intervention of Sutton's call, ordering Alex to disembark the aircraft at Zurich, caught him off guard.

"Whaddaya mean, get off the plane!?!" Alex exclaimed incredulously.

"I've changed my mind Alex, you're spending a week's briefing in Kashmir. Pick up your tickets at the Swiss counter. They've got your press passes, itinerary and work schedule … touch base when you get there!" Sutton barked, cutting him off.

His life with CMS had been a super-charged marathon. Running like a wildcat from one posting to another had been exhilarating. Nevertheless, the stark realities of living in war-torn countries had begun to take its toll. He was tired. He had had enough of running. Dodging dynamite and ducking grenades had become a way of life. Living with terror in one misery-wracked country only to be reassigned to another, had weakened his ability to think clearly about his personal life and future with Paris. His ideals, his conviction that the world could change, died, and his daring crusades amid human suffering and death became an all-too-vivid nightmare.

Opening the overhead locker to retrieve his camera bag, he moved to the tightly-secured cabin doors. Initially apologizing profusely for the inconvenience, he finally lost his temper when the pilot refused to disembark him. After a heated discussion, to his relief he was removed from the plane. The flight to Baghdad was delayed for two more hours after Alex caused it to miss its scheduled departure slot. Later, on board the flight to New Delhi, Alex thought about Paris, but at the back of his mind this seemed futile, as futile as his own life had been.

Alex knew it was wild to try to follow Paris but he had to do it. He had to return to her home to be with her once again. When Paris had left St. Moritz he had expected to forget her. He thought he would be able to carry on, even become someone else. Alex wanted to be a man who could love another woman, but however hard he tried he couldn't quite get her out of his mind. It surprised him to realise that he was desperate to be with her once again. Alex was astonished by his desire to hold Paris in his arms and to say he was sorry for not confessing his love to her. He was desperate to make love to her and to physically make their passion real. And now he couldn't forgive himself for not asking for her hand in marriage. *Why couldn't I take the plunge*, he chided himself. Alex had made errors in the past and many times he had longed to go back and do things differently. *How could he have let her go?* A woman like Paris, he knew he would never find again. He closed his eyes thinking about her. Alex realised only now he was hopelessly in love with her.

A week later, driving with relative ease through lax army checkpoints, passing sloping green meadows blooming with pink blossoms of apple and apricot trees, Alex was at last on the road to Sambara in search of Paris. Sutton's new work schedule had resulted in spending a gruelling first week in Srinigar. All Alex could think about was getting to her as fast as he could. Luckily, Sutton had also ordered him to go and get as many shots as possible of the "quaint" village clinic, Paris's home! *Hardly a hardship posting*, he grinned, with much admiration for his boss.

Following Paris was crazy, but letting her out from under his wing was much worse and forgetting her was impossible. He decided that now was the time to declare his undying love and openly show his affection. He could not get her out of his mind.

Full of doubt, Alex weighed the pros and cons of falling in love as he drove down the narrow road through the valley of Surinsar on his way to Sambara. As he came to the end of the valley opening up to yet another, he saw the dramatic view of the mountain ranges of Kashmir. He pulled over to the side of the road. The tidal wave of snowy peaks of the Himalayan range sharpened all his senses. Gazing at their majesty, he began to find the strength to search his own feelings deeply. Their beauty filled him with vitality. They not only captured his imagination but gave him with hope. He knew he could never forget this moment. He felt alive, he felt like a new man -- but he wondered how long this elation would last.

Parking under an apple tree, Alex changed into his hiking boots. Making his way down to the ravine, towards a stream, he selected a dry spot to pitch his tent. The receding snow patches and mild spring climate, relaxed him. Pitching his tent, he built a small fire close by. Settling down at sunset, after a wholesome meal of canned fish, baked potatoes, oranges and apricots plucked from the trees in the meadows, he again read the poem Paris had left in his jacket pocket in St. Moritz. He couldn't get her words out of his mind. *I have never had a passion so strong, nothing in my heart has lasted so long.* Feeling deeply anguished he recollected the secrets surrounding Malamar during an intimate conversation he had had with her father the night before they had left for Switzerland two years ago. As the dilemma of Paris's childhood became abundantly clear, he was again overwhelmed with a sense of loss. Since he tackled life like a bulldozer, never stopping to look around, never heeding advice, he buried his head in his hands, engulfed by a dread of losing her forever. Adding to his misery, Alex began to regret his unwillingness to accept Paris's criticisms. He wished he had listened to her. She was the only one who understood him. She knew how he felt and why he was a "complicated romantic" as she called him. Paris would say that he had the face of a thousand dreams. *You conceal, you conceal that is all I can feel --* he read on, silently, with only himself to blame.

Darkness fell and Alex had just enough time to clear up and settle down for the night. How many times had he read the poem, he asked himself. Settling down under the stars, he looked up into the night sky. *There was nowhere else in the world where one could see the heavens as clearly as here in the Himalayas,* he reflected. He cast his mind back to the events of the day, his travels through the peaceful villages that dotted the sloping meadows. Alex and his car had not perturbed the villagers; *on the contrary,* he mused, *it had more than delighted them. They appeared peaceful and content. Perhaps this was the best way to live, away from the modern world?* He read on. *You do not love me and you do -- you do not hate me and you do --* closing his eyes, he remembered the first day he had met Paris, their first embrace.

Two years earlier, Alex had joined a crew of wide-screen cinematographers in Kashmir. Their mission had been to film the climb to Mt. Surinsar for mountaineers across the world. The film crew responsible for hauling along a camera package, which when loaded with film magazines weighed more that forty-five pounds, had requested that CMS release Alex to head the team. In addition to filming the climbers, his job was to report on the technical and engineering aspects that enabled filming at excruciating sub-zero temperatures.

Alex had long been fascinated by the exploration of the Himalayan peaks and the dramatic stories of heroism and human achievement set against insurmountable odds. Just some years before he had acted as co-director for a crew filming expeditions to Everest. Since then, he had carefully studied a collection of climbing films, which he found to be limited in their ability to capture the lushness of the Himalayan range and the great spectacle of people climbing them. When Sutton Pearce had contacted him to head the crew in Kashmir, he had seized the opportunity.

In Sutton's mind, Alex had been the obvious choice. A fit man and a keen mountaineer, he was always game for a challenge. Moreover, his knowledge and experience of wide-screen technology was masterful.

On the previous film trip to the Himalayas, Alex as co-director discovered that writing a large-format documentary film was nothing like a normal video shoot. Because the camera is so heavy, the set-ups so complex, and the film itself so expensive, he could only plan limited shots. With this in mind, he was able to put together, for the Mt. Surinsar crew, a work schedule which guaranteed great footage during the climb.

Alex joined the crew along the Tawi river, where they had set up the base camp. The journey to the summit lasted many days. The crew were met with heavy snowfall, avalanches, and temperatures so cold that two of the crew were unable to continue. Eventually, against all odds, they reached the summit. As the shoot ended and the crew moved out of the area, Alex decided to stay onto rest. The flowing adrenaline of the last few months had faded leaving him exhausted and burned out. The prospect of going back to CMS and Switzerland filled him with apprehension as he realized he had become taken with the fairy-tale Himalayan countryside, making it almost impossible to draw himself away. *Enough of snowy peaks,* he thought, *it's time to explore green pastures and lie in wide meadows under the fiery stars at night, instead of freezing in a base camp on the edge of treacherous glaciers.*

In spite of the warnings of military intervention and the danger it imposed on every foreigner in the region, he hired a car with a driver, setting off to explore the homeland of the Kashmiri peoples. Nonetheless, Alex remained vigilant. His car, a cream-coloured Ambassador, capable of cruising only at a top speed of 60 mph, was chauffeur driven by the amiable Mr. Patel. Born in Vaduz on the Swiss border, Alex, a witty individual with a keen sense of humour, spent the first few days with the droll Mr. Patel travelling through the foothills of the Himalayas. Journeying through Kashmir, they scouted striking valleys, deep ravines and spectacularly scenic crevasses together. The gushing waterfalls and fast-flowing rapids, set against the backdrop of the Himalayan range was truly epic, and here Alex felt, he had found his paradise.

Mr. Patel, driver, citizen and sole companion, tackled the one-lane hairpin bends, cattle crossings, decrepit lorries, buses, and cyclists with brilliant adeptness. He navigated the Ambassador with skilful control. Once, Alex believed all was lost when their car swerved dangerously to the side of a threatening cornice. He later remarked *that if Mr. Patel had lost control of the steering wheel or swerved even slightly to the side, they would have plunged airborne into an unfathomable valley below.* Alex, only too aware of the danger, comforted himself by joking with Mr. Patel that if they should ever "take the plunge," his hang-glider moustache would flap them to safety, saving them both. Mr. Patel laughed out aloud in appreciation, nodding his head vehemently, clearly not *entirely* amused. However, he continued driving with great concentration, intent on keeping them both safe, and well away from a host of known as well as unanticipated dangers.

North of Surinsar, at a remote hill station dug into the hillside, Alex decided it was time to stay put for a while. He asked the warm-hearted Mr. Patel to make sleeping arrangements for them both at a respectable establishment. Mr. Patel nodded extravagantly and hurried away, leaving Alex to take in the balmy ambience of impending spring. When Mr. Patel finally returned, they got back in the car and headed for "a most respectable lodging." Mr. Patel politely informed Alex that the hotel of their destination had once been the summer home of a royal family from a bygone era. Now, he told him, it had fallen into the hands of the Indian army.

"Most respectable." Mr. Patel assured Alex again as they ventured further.

The village crammed alongside constricted streets had a raffish, bohemian ambience that was curiously engaging. Each panoramic view was intoxicating and the odour of burning wood permeated the air from every home. Delighted at Mr. Patel's *gem of a find*, Alex was further impressed when he could not locate the village on his map. "Conveniently omitted in order to avoid an influx of unbearable tourists, no doubt," he declared to Mr. Patel, who agreed instantly with a raised eyebrow and a fleeting grin. Alex registered them both into the Quarters Hotel where Alex's room looked out over fields of reddish-yellow poppies.

Alex's bedroom overflowed with stuffed deer heads. A small mahogany bed, an immense Victorian armchair and a heavily polished writing desk filled the small room. A huge gilt-framed mirror, "left behind by Queen Victoria, no doubt," Alex joked to Mr. Patel, who was clearly not impressed, occupied the panel above the fireplace. A fire burned as Alex sat without a book, without a drink -- with only his thoughts to entertain him.

Later that evening, dinner over, Alex spent an amusing moment with Mr. Patel, who kept Alex's glass topped up with whisky. As Alex headed back to the two steps leading to his room, he failed to notice the last step was twice the height of the previous ones. Buckling his ankle at a 90-degree angle, he fell to the floor in agony. The twist was so painful he let out a roar. Two hotel employees appeared out of nowhere and helped him to his room. Mr. Patel ran to his aid also, offering another glass of whisky to dull the pain.

"A most unfortunate move!" he said dryly, lifting Alex onto his bed.

Half an hour later, when Alex saw that his right ankle had swollen to three times the size of its counterpart, he rang for help. It arrived in the shape of a diminutive old man with pearly eyes of wisdom, shoulder length grey hair and bushy eyebrows, holding a staff with one hand and a bottle in the other. Along with him came his beautiful young assistant.

The doctor, robed in a long brown tunic, tied at the waist, had been summoned from the village clinic, which Alex later discovered, was a tiny room located in the bazaar behind an old English bookstore. His assistant, Alex guessed, was probably in her late teens. Even in his debilitated state he noticed her skin was a superb olive-ivory depending on the light, and her black hair flowed about her shoulders.

"Mr. Alex Vadim?" the doctor inquired. Alex, red faced and grimacing, nodded his head morosely.

"That's me," he groaned gripping his knee as the pain shot up his leg.

"I have come to help you," he said, pouring a greyish gelatinous liquid onto a clean rag. *Thank goodness, at least the rag is clean*, Alex thought, as he began to tremble.

The doctor dribbled a copious amount of the greyish liquid onto Alex's swollen ankle and then massaged his foot with honey salve from a lavender smelling bottle. The slightest touch sent shock waves of pain up his leg. Before he could complain, the doctor grabbed the heel of his ankle with one hand, the toes with the other and began to twist it hard against the sprain. Alex screamed wildly. The assistant stepped forward and held him down as the doctor continued to massage the painful swelling. Alex screamed, begging for mercy. The assistant disappeared into the bathroom and emerged with a bucket of ice cold water and plunged his foot into it. Alex yelled and held onto the girl's arm for fear of fainting on the spot. Then, after removing his foot from the glacial ice water, she dried it with the rag, massaged it with more honey salve, gently pushed Alex back down on the bed where he lay feeling exhausted and stupefied.

The girl, enveloped in a black woollen salwa kameez, spoke. "You have a bad sprain."

As if I didn't know, he nearly blurted out cynically, regretting the thought instantly. He was surprised to hear beautifully spoken English so far away from home.

"Er, you speak English ... perfectly," he stuttered, feeling a fool for saying it.

Damn it, he thought, *why do I always act like an idiot where women are concerned.* The girl continued to massage his foot gently, careful not to injure it further. A few minutes later she turned to the doctor and mumbled something in the local dialect.

"You should be able to walk later today. Get up and try to walk in about an hour. There should be little pain. Take it easy for a few days. My father says you should not continue your journey until you are completely recovered. Perhaps in a week's time," she concluded.

"Where did you learn to speak such good English?" Alex inquired as he gripped onto the side of the bed to haul himself upright. He wondered why he kept repeating himself. Afraid she would disappear and he would never see her again, he felt a sudden urge to know everything about her.

"Here in Jammu Kashmir. English is my first language. I learned it before I was five years old. But I do speak the local dialect."

"Yes, I heard. So the doctor's your dad?" Alex said, hoping he didn't sound like a dying man who had just put his foot in it. He winced to himself at the pun. Then he wondered whether he sounded like a hotshot frantic journalist asking the right questions at the right time and in the right order. After all, he told himself, he was not preparing a script for a local shoot. He tried to relax.

"Yes, he's the local doctor. Our village is small and difficult to get to, so we cannot rely on doctors from the big towns. Srinigar is more than a hundred miles from here. Jammu is much closer, but our roads are in bad condition and the cliffs are dangerous, so not many doctors want to come to Sambara. We fend for ourselves and the local people are highly experienced in crafts." She wrinkled her nose as she smiled, and Alex felt his heart melting, until the pain in his ankle started to throb again.

"Don't worry about your foot. My father has cured more sprained ankles than you can count poppies in the meadows, and we have millions of them here! You're not the first one to sprain an ankle, you know. It happens all the time - as you can see from the terrain, it's very easy to do so. But it's normally outdoors, not indoors," she said, poking fun at him.

"You'll be well soon. My father's an expert in these matters," she continued as she walked over to him and held out her hand. "Here, hold my hand and try to get up."

Taking her hand, Alex pulled himself up. Leaning against her for support, he slowly put his foot on the floor, twitching in immeasurable pain. Firmly gripping his hand, she helped Alex hobble to the bathroom. To his surprise, the sharp pains in his foot began to ease and in little time he was able to walk back and forth on his own, but the burning sensation was nevertheless very present. The doctor, his back turned, said something to the girl as she gathered up their belongings to leave.

"That'll be five rupees please," she said to Alex.

Alex, aghast, nearly fell over again. *Only five rupees for a cure. It was scandalous,* he thought, realizing he had not completely recovered.

"Are you sure?" he mumbled, feeling humiliated. "Are you sure it's enough? I can pay more," he offered.

"No, that's the going rate. My father does not charge tourists more. The rate is five rupees, please."

Alex grabbed his jacket and fumbled around for a five-rupee note, ashamed his manner could have offended them. *Why was it easier to pay big bucks in big cities than small bucks in small villages,* he asked himself. The world to him seemed upside down and inside out. Alex could not make heads or tails of it. He wanted to pay more, lots more, but he knew that it would not be accepted. *These people were different,* he thought, *and money had a different value and a different meaning. Here it was simply paper. It meant surviving but not survival.* Alex paid the modest doctor, who bowed upon receiving the money and left with his daughter as abruptly as he had appeared with her.

Alex slumped back to catch his breath, thinking about the girl. He could not get her dark almond eyes out of his mind. *If only I could get her telephone number. Oh God, she probably doesn't have a phone. Or, I'll just get her address, but she probably wouldn't give it to me*, he debated, lost in his own thoughts. Then, without further delay, Alex hopped in agony to the door like a kangaroo, clutching onto it for support as he yelled after them.

"Could you ask your father to come back and examine my foot again? Tomorrow?" his voice shrilled excitedly. "I'd be willing to pay," he added, cursing himself seconds later for being so crass. *Damnation, I've put my foot in it again*, he thought, as he cringed. Moments later, the girl nimbly raced up the two unevenly shaped steps to his room, coming face to face with him. Alex looked into her dark eyes and knew he was falling in love with her.

"Hello again, he'll be back in the morning," she informed him softly.

"Will you come with him?"

"Yes, until tomorrow then," she said hastily.

"What time?" he pressed her earnestly.

"Early!"

"How early?" Alex said feeling his foot smarting again.

"9?"

"Great, thanks," he concluded, rubbing the soreness gently with his fingertips wondering whether he could wait that long to see her again.

Alex leaned against the door, trembling with deep excitement, trying to remember when he had felt like this before, realizing that he never had. Staring into the blazing fireplace, he hobbled toward it to throw more logs on and then took two giant hops to the window. A horse-drawn carriage carrying the doctor and his daughter looked engagingly romantic against the striking background of manicured hills. The girl in the carriage reinvigorated Alex so keenly that he could no longer imagine leaving the tiny village the following day or the next. As the carriage pulled away, his knees buckled as he watched her long sleek hair blowing in the wind. Swiftly grabbing his camera, Alex instinctively began to shoot them from his window. Later that night, he realized that he had not only fallen desperately in love, but also that he had no idea where he was. To make matters worse, he reflected, he did not know her name.

The next morning Alex, unable to sleep was up well before six waiting in suspense for their promised arrival. The ailing foot no longer had the appearance of raw meat and the swelling had almost disappeared. He was still unable to put much pressure on it and spent most of the morning in pain, as he perfected his hopping technique to appear more in control.

At exactly two seconds past nine, Alex hopped to the wooden door when he heard a faint knock. As he swung it open, he was surprised to see the girl unaccompanied. Elated, Alex thanked the gods for this opportunity to get to know her better. Tall slim, she looked seductively innocent. Alex noticed that she found him amusing and this made him feel like an idiot again, but he was prepared to put up with it. After all, he told himself, he was at her mercy. Anyway, he argued, since she was taking care of him it seemed apt that she should have some fun while she was fussing over his wounded ankle.

"I'm so glad you're here … the foot's still pretty bad … guess I'll be needing a lot more treatment. Could take days before I'm outta here … would you like to come in?" Alex rambled.

A man who normally despised small talk, Alex found himself doing the same. He lay on his bed while the girl massaged his tender foot with the honey salve. After several moments of hell he let out a raucous yelp and turned sanguine. Plucking up enough courage to continue the small talk and camouflage his pain, he decided to put possible romance into motion.

"Look … er … oouch … I'd like to stick around here for a while … what's fun to oooh … watch out! … oooh … do around here?" he shrieked as she rubbed his foot with soft even strokes. "I have a driver so I don't intend to … ouch … walk too much."

Covering his foot with a cool compress, she left it for a while. Alex took some deep breaths and began to relax until moments later, to his horror she began to administer more of the honey salve. He flinched several times as she worked gently on the ankle, massaging up to his knee.

"How does that feel now?" she asked sympathetically.

"Much … ooch … better … really … just you being here makes me feel a whole lot better … it still … ooch … hurts but your dad worked miracles on me last night and I'm very grateful," Alex whimpered.

"He heals with his faith," the girl explained, as she bandaged his foot.

Alex feeling vulnerable and bleak wondered if he had any faith at all. When the girl finally smiled at him he detected an unusual majestic presence that touched him deeply. In fact, Alex realised, it made him feel unworthy of her. Stunned by his own ability to feel so deeply, so quickly, he avoided thinking about it further and concentrated on his sore ankle, deciding that it was far easier to deal with than love. Moreover, he noticed, that besides the deep excitement and sense of possibility tearing him apart, he also had a palpable urge to play with her hair. *Is this it*, Alex wondered, *is this love?*

Loving, Alex brooded pessimistically, was normally over in a matter of days. Women had always intrigued him but he had never fallen in love. There was something else about Paris which made a long-lasting impression. It was her aura of genteel nobility. That, he surmised, could be very intimidating. If there was ever a woman to die for, he imagined Paris had to be the one. She was worth every emotion, every heartbeat, every ounce of air he could breathe. He was sure he could love her.

Lying awake beneath the deep blue sky at night, Alex dreamed about Paris. Gazing into its deep void, he counted legions of shooting stars appearing from all corners of the universe. It was time to sleep as he had exhausted himself. Wearily he stamped out the last persistent cinders, picked up his blanket and retreated into the tent. Paris had captured his heart, leaving him tossing and turning while his mind battled with a multitude of fond memories and turbulent thoughts. Alex poured himself a stiff drink and tried again to sleep. Finally, in the early hours of the morning, when the northerly wind had calmed, he slept too.

9

The Gold Box

When the doctor's daughter first saw Alex, she could hardly take her eyes off him as he lay helpless on the bed at the Quarters Hotel. His thick golden hair and muscular body sent quivers through. Falling in love was something that she had conveniently avoided during her college years, concentrating more on her studies than romance. During the three years she spent at the University of Srinigar she had been constantly showered with gifts and wooed by some of the most eligible men at the university, but none had captured her heart. Now she was face to face with someone who could not take his eyes off her and she, for the first time, felt a warmth so tender, so endearing that she wondered whether this could be love. The girl glanced at her father nervously, wondering whether this astute, kind man could hear her throbbing heart and whether he could sense her attraction to his handsome patient. While she assisted her father she reflected about how his devotion and care had changed her life, and she was not prepared to jeopardize this.

I wish he wouldn't stare at me like that, she thought repeatedly. But only because she wanted to stare back at him, study his features and memorize his distinguishing traits. As her heart pounded, she realized this was a man she could love. To justify these sudden feelings, she tried convincing herself that her reaction was purely physical. She diagnosed her dizziness, queasy stomach, weak knees and almost childish behaviour as signs of flu. *I must be coming down with something.*

As her father treated his foot and Alex winced with pain, she knew she would have to see him again. She gasped each time their eyes met that afternoon, ultimately admonishing the pleasure and rebuking his glances. This isn't love, she convinced herself, yet she could not draw herself away.

As her father realised the impact Alex was having on his daughter, he became even more protective, sending her on pointless missions to the bathroom to fill the bucket. Consequently, she did something very out of character, she practiced restraint. But all she really wanted to think about was his well formed body, his remarkable sea-green eyes and skin seductively bronzed from the snow and sun. She massaged his foot and with every touch they bonded.

Neither father nor daughter spoke much during the horse-drawn carriage ride back to the clinic. Directly overhead, they spotted a V-configuration of geese migrating over the Himalayas. The flock appeared almost motionless passing high above them. Then came the spine-chilling echoes of the last of the rumbling, billowing avalanches where huge chunks of ice unpredictably peeled off the Surinsar wall and came crashing down. Unperturbed, the horse strutted to the pleasing aroma of juniper incense burning at a nearby temple. Moments later, they passed a variety of primroses. Yellow cinquefoils poked out of the crevices in the trail and tiny lavender-blue butterflies twirled in spirals. Along the trail to the clinic azaleas bloomed alongside magnolias. A herd of deer grazed in the paddocks on route.

The doctor's misery was his daughter's nightmare. How was she ever going to leave home? A dilemma, until now, she had managed to put aside. She could sense his concern and she had clearly registered his alarm in the Quarters Hotel.

Later that evening, carrying several butter lamps with twisted cotton wicks, the girl entered the humble dwelling where her father sat in an armchair cloaked in maroon brocade robes. The dimly lit room was barely large enough to hold a table, let alone a visitor. Now an aged man, the doctor sat pensively in front of a fire staring at the burning logs. She went to close the window as even the slightest breeze could have put out the wicks. A large raven believed to be the auspicious bearer of human souls, sat perched on his windowsill. Shooing it away, she closed the window and went to her father's side.

"Father, I love you with all my heart. I'm your daughter and whatever happens I will always love you."

He looked fixedly at her with sadness.

"Dearest daughter, you're a grown woman, you must do what your heart tells you. I caught you in my arms when the heavens opened and since, you have been my saviour. Your mother will be inconsolable when you leave. We love you very much. Nevertheless, I know that day will come. You will live your life to the fullest and we will be proud of you. I know you cannot look through a window without ever stepping outside. I hope that whatever you wish, whatever you want, my dearest Angel, with God's grace you will have." After some time, he spoke again. "You must go alone tomorrow and treat Mr. Alex. I am feeling very tired and I think my assistance will not be necessary. Go early and come back before the clinic opens." On that final note he gazed listlessly into the fire, seeking peace as the blaze burned down to a cinder. The girl put her arms around her father's neck and stayed close to him until she retired for the evening.

The next morning the girl was up early. She threw on a floppy sweater and jeans, wrapped herself in a large black shawl.

Her mother called out imperiously, "Tie your hair back or it will look untidy." As the excitement of seeing Alex mounted, she replied, "Mother, you know I never tie it back! Don't worry, I'm going to be fine. I'll be home before the clinic opens." The girl left home, excited and expectant.

Walking down the tiny back streets of Sambara, the girl stopped by a stream to pray at the Sarawasti temple. She bought sweets and garlands of marigolds for the tiny effigy of the angelic Goddess of Learning, carved in pristine marble. A few moments later she was following the trail of yellow cinquefoils to the hotel.

The Quarters Hotel, made entirely of wood, resembled a quintessentially English country cottage. The front garden cultivated evergreen shrubs abundantly and small clumps of dusky pink heather bloomed everywhere. Wearing flat, sensible shoes she climbed the two steps hearing every squeak, taking care not to trip where Alex had. The dilapidated steps sagged unevenly in disrepair and she understood how easily Alex could have misjudged their size. The girl knocked on the door. A second later, Alex opened it and welcomed her. The happiness on his face brightened up her day, eased her nervousness and settled the butterflies in her stomach.

The girl tended to his foot with professional detachment. In the process, she avoided his persistent gaze. She filled the bucket with hot water, bathed and dried his foot. Then she proceeded to massage the swollen ankle with the honey salve and bandaged it in soft muslin. When he tried to strike up a conversation, she avoided responding. When he obliquely suggested they get together, to Alex's distress, she appeared uninterested. She avoided his stare and when he said anything at all, she remained silent. But deep down inside she was desperate to hold him, and for the first time ever, she had the irresistible urge to tell him all her secrets. At the end of twenty minutes or so, she returned to her father's clinic, leaving Alex alone to savour the pleasure of having been with her.

The excitement of seeing her again left Alex exhausted, very quickly he fell asleep. He woke an hour later to find himself feeling a whole lot better. Alex couldn't get the image of this sultry girl out of his head. He limped to the bathroom and splashed his face with icy cold water. It felt like melted snow. It woke him up completely with a shudder and suddenly he felt on the top of the world. *Could this be bliss?* Alex reflected. Just the thought of this woman made him happy. Each time he thought of her massaging his foot with her soft hands, he felt elated. *Her persona,* he mused *was as magical as the green pastures of the countryside.* He felt he was living in a fairytale. *Crazy thoughts, write them down, don't forget them,* he concluded. Moments later, he found himself hopping madly to the window and marvelling at the sight of antelopes. A small, grey and brown one wandered close to his window. Alex began to wonder how odd it looked with its backward curving horns and long wispy hair. The sight of it amused him.

Alex stayed indoors for the rest of the day. As the pain faded and dusk finally fell, Mr. Patel joined him for dinner only this time they ate in Alex's room.

☙☙☙

The next day, Alex woke up very early to a bitterly cold morning and a brilliant sun just rising over the amphitheatre of the Himalayas. The bluest of blue skies and its over-spilling luminosity filled his room. He inspected his healing, but still tender ankle.

Invigorated under a shower of glacial water from gorges nearby, he dressed feeling inexplicably animated and refreshed. Alex grabbed his camera and brooded about the doctor's daughter. He hopped out of his room skirting the sinister step of two nights before, and mastered the hallway leading to the dining room.

Alex ate a cheerful breakfast with Mr. Patel who effusively congratulated him on *his very very speedy recovery* and *his very very excellent appetite,* in spite of his *very very terrible ordeal* the day before. Mr. Patel, who feared Alex might well fall over again or worse still break his neck, repeatedly wished him *a very very good day* as he nervously stroked his elongated black moustache. Mr. Patel's unusual moustache appeared to have been doused in some sort of sticky gel, so Alex jokingly asked when he *planned to take off* or whether he was just trying to avoid *a crash landing*! Mr. Patel responded with a muffled laugh and then coughed discreetly, avoiding Alex's twinkling eyes. Mr. Patel soon pulled up in the car to take him to his destination.

For the first time since his arrival, with his camera on one shoulder and a walking stick in his hand, Alex left the Quarters Hotel. The hotel gardens evoked memories of his childhood as the lemony perfume of rhododendron permeated the air. Sitting in the back seat of the car with his leg outstretched comfortably, he reminisced about home in Vaduz, his family and his favourite companion, his trust-

148

worthy golden Labrador, Aspen, who liked to eat dinner napkins and drool on his nicest pair of trousers. He remembered the countryside around the cottage where he grew up. Alex began to miss the long walks there, wishing he could jog through the park with Aspen. He missed the people he loved the most, the people he had rarely had time for, he reflected with regret. *Did I ever appreciate any of it?* Alex scolded himself. Alex regretted that the simplest pleasures of life had passed him by. Why could he feel such a bond with his good-tempered and loving pet, and yet with women, he had not been able to feel the way he did now about the doctor's daughter, who had appeared like an angel in his time of need? Mr. Patel drove Alex down into the village. Alex caught up in the paradox of his life and his surroundings, took in the ambiance. *Today was a new day*, he told himself, *it could also be the start of a new life.*

They arrived at the English bookshop several minutes later. Above the shop, a dilapidated sign tilted precariously to one side, swaying in the wind. *Looking as if it was about to administer a severe knock to some unfortunate passer-by*, Alex thought, he pulled it down. The sign read "Village Clinic."

"Hey, whaya doin' …?" said a fretful voice pulling at Alex's sleeve. "Hey whaya doin'?" repeated the boy, a distraught skinny lad whose shiny cropped hair had been flattened with gel. Tugging at his sleeve again Alex noticed the boy's big ears and bright intelligent eyes. His walnut-coloured sweater, his baggy shorts, his swarthy complexion and knee-high woollen socks - Alex took it all in, still holding the broken sign, as the boy gaped at him.

"Why do that. Why?" the boy parroted on.

"Who are you?" inquired Alex, slightly irritated.

"That my sign, my shop, my sign!" he responded pointing to the wooden plaque in Alex's hand.

Alex spoke. "I'm Alex Vadim, I'm staying down at the Quarters hotel. I'll fix it and bring it back later. It could hurt someone if it falls down."

The dark-skinned boy made a face as if to say he had never noticed the broken sign and, even if he had, since it had always been like that, why change it?

"Please, please, please Mr. Alex, come this way."

Behind the bookshop was the village clinic. It consisted of two small rooms sparsely furnished. The waiting room was packed with patients huddled together near a heater. Tattered old *Vogue* magazines and Superman comics scattered over a coffee table made useful mats for hot sweet tea.

The patients sat on a blue plastic sofa like puppets. They clumped together like grapes on the vine. Next to the sofa stood a transparent partition. The far inside wall was lined with shelves of colourful pills, dry herbs, rainbow-coloured powders and potions all neatly labelled and in order. Above the bed that resembled a stretcher, was a shelf crammed full of honey jars. Stationery, prescriptions and a doctor's rubber stamps were neatly arranged next to a sign, "homeopathic surgery." Hanging on the other side of the wall were details of opening hours in both English and the local dialect. Alex followed the skinny boy who had returned to serve hot sweet tea from a large urn outside. As the boy served tea in saucers, the quaint little backroom became alive with gossip as if the patients were in a theatre anticipating the second act. The sounds of enjoyment, their splutters and slurps brought warmth into the unusual setting. Squatting outside the clinic, warming his hands on the hot urn, the boy patiently waited to take back his cups and saucers.

Meanwhile Alex, holding onto the sign, sat down to rest his sore ankle. Rummaging through the Superman comics, he noticed they were as old as he was, some even older. He examined the dates 1964, 1967, and 1972. They were so rare he could do nothing but let out a roar of laughter, much to the surprise of the other patients. He realized their value could easily pay for a large stock of medical supplies. He wondered whether he should mention to the doctor that these collector's items were worth more than their weight in gold.

The doctor's daughter emerged from the back room looking radiant. She was holding a pair of crutches. With a broad endearing smile, Alex greeted her.

"Good morning, I've been kidnapped by the boy."

"Oh, how's your foot ... er ... sorry ... he runs errands for my father!" she said.

"I took this sign down, I was going to make a new one and put it up tomorrow ... it was hanging off a nail. Thought it was dangerous unless you were hoping to increase your clientele," he joked.

She laughed and he confirmed, "You've hit the nail on the head." They cringed together at such a corny joke.

"Well okay, thanks," she said, "It's been hanging like that for quite awhile. No one takes any notice of it. It needed fixing so I'm sure my father will be very grateful to you," she said reassuringly. "How's the ankle?"

"Oh it's fine. You worked magic on it. I'm really grateful. I just came by to say thanks." He was nervous and wondered if it showed, trying desperately to keep the conversation alive and getting very little help.

"Look, I don't wish to pry, but I don't even know your name." *Maybe she doesn't have a name,* he thought. *Now don't be crazy*, he told himself, *everyone has a name.*

Glancing at an old *Vogue* magazine lying under some sticky comics, she came across a caption that read:

Paris Fashions, Explosive Winter Collection by

France's Greatest Pop Art Designer, Cassi di Svega

With an air of finality Alex chose not to contest she replied unflinchingly, "Paris, my name is Paris Cassidis."

Glimpsing the same magazine cover, Alex wondered why she could not divulge her real name. *I'm crazy about you*, he confessed to himself. Courteously, he responded, "I like it, yes I do. What a good solid name! Well … let me officially introduce myself. Alex Vadim … photojournalist for CMS … are the crutches for me?"

Later that afternoon, Alex returned to the village clinic on his crutches with a colourful new sign that he diligently hooked back up above the bookshop. He looked the scene over and felt proud, congratulating himself on a job well done, the arrow shape having been his idea. He mused about what it had taken to get the sign made, and mostly about Paris, until he heard the faint rumble of vehicles in the distance.

Paris, who had spotted Alex outside shouted at him.

"Get inside now!" she demanded.

Alex obeyed wondering what he had done wrong. *Didn't she like the sign? Perhaps the colours ...?*

She picked up his crutches and yanked him into the clinic at top speed. Minutes later a convoy of three jeeps snaked up the u-shaped arterial road leading toward the village. The grey-haired doctor wheeled aside the clinic bed and pried opened a concealed trap door leading to a crawl space below. Briskly, he shoved Alex and Paris inside as the ruckus of honking came clearly into earshot.

"I'll explain later," the doctor murmured urgently to Alex, "but, whatever you do, whatever you see, please *do not try to get out.*"

"I will come and get you when it is safe but now it is very dangerous for you both to be seen." He slammed the trap door shut with his foot, rolling the bed over it. The doctor put on a padded sleeveless jacket. He concealed it under his white coat.

Rays of light mercifully streamed through the cracks in the floor. Alex, not able to navigate on the steps, slipped and landed heavily on his back. Wincing as the pain shot up his leg, he gripped his knee in anguish.

He lowered his voice, "Who are they ... terrorists? I can look after myself. I've been through this kind of thing before." He spoke in hushed tones.

"Ssshh ..." she cautioned, "I know. Stay still and quiet or you'll get us all in trouble," Paris whispered, biting her nails and trembling with fear.

The vehicles boomed to the Quarters Hotel to load crates of distilled gin made from local juniper berries. Several minutes later, they roared past the paddocks, through the main bustling throughway and screeched to a halt outside the clinic.

The shadowy hole brimming with medical supplies was half Alex's height and barely the width of his outstretched arms. Squashed together on a splintery step they waited in chilled silence as the men tore into the waiting room. Next, they proceeded to kick down the door and burst into the doctor's surgery.

Through slits of the floorboards, Alex eyed three men in khaki uniforms holding rifles while interrogating the doctor. Paris, frozen with fear, moved closer to Alex gesturing to him to stay as still as possible. One soldier shoved the doctor onto a stool knocking his staff out of his hand and into the air. It landed spinning and clacking over the concealed door. Another soldier began to jab him in the back remorselessly. Through the slit, Alex could make out the doctor's perspiring face. The third man tied his ankles to the stool and viciously struck him again on his back and booted him to the floor. His lifeless body lay crumpled there while the men looked on, seething with frustration as the doctor had refused to talk. The need to defend the helpless, mixed with guilt, at his inaction, overcame Alex.

"That's it, Paris, I'm getting out to help your father … I've had enough I can't stay here any longer!" he whispered agonizingly.

Paris gripped him hard.

"No, don't move … you'll make matters worse," she begged.

"Well … what is it they want … for Christ's sake …?" he muttered through fiercely clenched teeth.

"You!"

"Me … why me?" Alex whispered angrily under the din as his nostrils flared.

"Sssshh, please" Paris begged again. "'Cause you're a foreigner … word must have got round … that … sshhh!" She pleaded softly.

"So you mean *I'm* the cause of this?" he gestured incredulously, feeling more guilty.

The doctor lay on the floor close to his staff. His eyes opened and closed.

The incensed men plundered the clinic, swiping the supplies they did not want onto the floor with their rifle butts. They threw the other supplies into the back of their three-vehicle convoy and left suddenly, following the road down into the valley.

It wasn't until they had long been out of earshot, that Paris loosened her grip on Alex. In tears, she clambered out of the cellar to go to her father's aid. The old but sturdy doctor, weakened by the blow, lay tied to the stool. Alex, burning with anger, untied him and carried him to the bed. Her father managed to utter few consoling words to Paris, who was unable to control her tears.

"You are safe … you are safe … that's all that counts." The doctor muttered as Paris examined him carefully before soothing his forehead with honey salve. Finally, the doctor fell asleep.

"How old is he?" Alex asked suddenly.

"Sixty-eight or thereabouts. Birthdays were never recorded at that time."

"Will he be alright … I'm so sorry I couldn't help … I feel …"

"Alex, you did the right thing … if you had helped him, you would have implicated us all. I've just covered his wounds with the same salve that healed your foot … it has healing properties."

"It sure worked wonders … how's he doing … will he be alright?" Alex asked again.

"Yes, he just needs to rest. Look … here, he put thick padding under his coat … we've been through this sort of thing before," she said, tears still streaming down her cheeks.

Alex opened his arms and she fell into his comforting embrace. Her heartbeat quickened as he enveloped her into his hold.

"You should leave soon, its dangerous here." Paris said earnestly, "The colour of your hair is just too big a give-away!"

"I'm sorry I've caused you all this trouble," Alex confessed, still chilled from the cruel spectacle.

Paris shivered in his arms.

Alex said, "I know India and Pakistan have been at log-gerheads over Kashmir, but … I'll be honest with you … I never expected to see this first hand," he confessed.

Paris inquired, "You must know how dangerous it is?"

"Yes, I do, I guess that's what kept me in the cellar, knowing that if I got out what it would do to you and the rest of your family. I'm truly sorry! Who were those guys? They weren't speaking the local lingo!"

"I don't know," Paris said as Alex wiped away her tears. Alex held her closer and stroked her face and hair lovingly, "All we know is that they are barbarians and blood turns them on. We live in a lawless land without borders!"

"How did they know I was here?"

"Who knows? Normally they come and take medical supplies. I've never shown my face. I always go down into the cellar to hide. It's a perfect hiding spot."

"You mean they've done this kind of thing to your father before?"

"Yes, it happens all the time, they rough the place up and leave. Today was particularly bad because someone must have sent word that a foreign journalist was in town. If they'd seen you here they'd have held us all hostage!"

Alex added, "I heard that only last week they shot an innocent tourist. He'd been held captive for months in the caves along the Surinsar wall. These men think only with their weapons. It seems they don't care who they kill or why, almost enjoying fighting other people's battles for money, greed or political reasons."

They sat together for a while in each other's arms. Alex experienced a deep empathy he had never felt before, and Paris felt dazed, knowing all too well this beginning could be the end. He released his grip and went over to hold the doctor's hand.

"How is he?" Alex asked again feeling responsible.

"He's sleeping, no broken bones and hopefully not too many bruises either, thank God. He's old now, it'll take a day or two to heal and get over the shock, I'm afraid."

"Why do you stay? It's dangerous here for you and your family."

"It's our home! We'd never leave ... but *you* must! It's too dangerous for you to stay in Sambara any longer."

"I'm not leaving without you," Alex suddenly found himself saying. Paris fell silent. He pulled her closer, shielding her again with his broad strong shoulders.

CAGAD

Two days passed before Alex saw Paris again. On the first day, high winds moved in over the isolated village of Sambara. This created huge pockets of water-saturated clouds, which resulted in unstoppable rain. Thick clouds raced passed the Trikuta range and biting gales scoured the Surinsar wall emitting another distant and ominous roar. On the second morning fog settled over the village. Alex, unable to get Paris out of his mind, sent a note through Mr. Patel inquiring after her father's health. When a note came back thanking him for his concern, reassuring him that the doctor's health was improving and that the clinic would reopen the following morning, he sent Paris a dinner invitation. She accepted. Now fully recovered, Alex greeted Paris with both feet firmly on the ground.

During dinner, Alex asked Paris why the situation in Kashmir could not be resolved amicably. There was profound sadness in her voice.

"You see, before partition, Kashmir used to be a princely state. The Maharaja, a Hindu, ruled over a predominantly Muslim population, hoping to remain independent of either."

"So what happened to him?" Alex asked.

"After partition he delayed his decision to accede to either Pakistan or India hoping to achieve independence for his principality. Then, to his surprise, the land was brutally invaded by tribesmen from the northwest frontier province."

"And?"

"And … well, the Maharaja fearing for his life finally agreed to accede to the Indian dominion, partly to gain Indian military assistance against a possible revolt."

"Why don't the people of Kashmir just vote which way they want to go?" Alex asked.

She responded, "They tried back in '65 and '72! The people even demanded a UN-supervised referendum, but India refused."

"So which side were the soldiers at the clinic on?"

"Neither, they're terrorists!" she continued, "the men you saw are based near the mysterious ruins of Mahora Gahat near the front line of control."

"Tell me, Paris … how on earth do we define a terrorist? Surely, these people are fighting for a cause they believe in."

"It's a good question," she responded. "There's a great deal of disagreement over how to differentiate between terrorists and those who fight to rid their nation of foreign occupiers. I used to run an underground newsletter in Srinigar known as Sidelines which tried to give all points of view. While I was at the university we operated from an abandoned basement. I was the photographer - that's my specialty! It was fun and rewarding, but too dangerous. My father wants me to leave and I will, when the time comes."

Alex fell silent and looked her in the eyes, wondering whether he was being too hasty and risked scaring her away.

"I'm impressed! Come to Europe with me and join CMS. We're always looking for promising young people. You'll see the world and cover other conflicts ... you can't fight your own wars, you know."

"Thanks for the offer but I have to consider my parents."

"Think about it. The offer stands. I'll arrange to get you out. All you have to do is say yes."

For Alex his feelings for Paris had not only been fuelled by her rare beauty, he had also sensed an air of sophistication almost aristocratic. Her devotion to her family had impressed him and left him longing for his own. Her ability to believe that the impossible was possible had cut through his cynical perception of life. Her exquisite refinement not only fired his imagination but sparked his readiness to give up his heart. After dinner, Paris left the Quarters Hotel knowing what her decision was going to be.

When Paris arrived home she went to her father's room. He sat alone fighting back tears as the fire began to die down. She entered with a tray of butter lamps and a large cup of sweet tea. As Paris sat at her father's feet, watching him sip his tea, she realized he was a man of sacrifice. Her father was a wise man who cared nothing for material comfort. A calm man who could be respected. She smiled at him. He was holding a gold box inlaid with rice pearls. He held the box out for her to take. She hesitated, wondering what it could mean. Opening the box she saw a breathtaking ruby necklace. She started to tremble. Tears rolled down her cheeks. He spoke quietly.

"Your life is in this box." He gave her a letter, which she read.

The mystery of this gold box is in your heart. Let your imagination twirl and close your eyes. Imagine you are far away from all that exists and think of treasures of gold, islands of paradise, warm lagoons upon your feet. Inside this treasure chest, you will find all these pleasures, all these desires. As you open it, it will be your source of life, your dreams, your wishes. It will be your heart and soul as with one action of your hand you will be showered with the golden dust of life. Let no evil find its place. For then you will crumble and lose face. Open your mind and body and let yourself go deep into your heart. Breathe so deeply that you can hardly move and let the air around you spin into a frenzy of freedom. The embedded pearls will be the paths you choose and each of them will make your fantasies real. Choose what you will but never with greed and all your dreams will come true. Give yourself to friend and foe. Give to them your sincerity. Look into the box and tell me what you can see. Look carefully beyond into the depths of the seas. For there lies a secret for all of us to find, as your life as you have it is all in your mind.

After midnight, the doctor left the clinic alone, in a horse-drawn carriage. He headed toward the Quarters Hotel. He had been very determined and nothing would change his mind.

"Keta, don't go, please don't go. It is too late and you are still too weak … please don't upset the photographer!" his wife Seetha had cautioned. But he did not respond. He was bent on seeing Alex. He put on his woollen hat, wrapped himself in a heavy coat and set off to the Quarters Hotel.

Alex, in his pyjamas, opened his door to the penetrating gaze of Paris's father. He was shocked to see him. *What was he doing here*, Alex mused before welcoming him in and offering a seat. The doctor remained standing. Alex decided to sit.

"Mr. Alex, may I ask you your age?"

"Yes, twenty-seven." Alex replied.

"My daughter is twenty-one." Alex bit his lip and nodded. There was silence between them.

"My daughter came to see you this evening. She is a very resolute lady, you know." She tells me that you wish her to go to Europe and work in your … *job!* This is good news. She is an intelligent girl. She will be an asset to any one who gives her employment."

The doctor paused thoughtfully, as if arranging his thoughts so that he would say the right words in the correct order and not mislead Alex in any way. He was a careful man and to be misunderstood was not his goal. He walked across the room and rested his staff against the wall. He took a deep breath and tried to relax. He was tired, his mind exhausted, his muscles weak from the ordeal just days before. He sat down with a purpose. He proceeded to tell Alex the story. The story he had so deeply dreaded he would someday be obliged to divulge. He spoke of how he had found his daughter falling from the skies, of how he had nursed her back to health. The doctor continued by recounting the myth of Malamar, Paris's flight to freedom, the promise, her heritage, her royal blood and the sanctity of marriage. He pierced Alex's heart.

"This cannot be true, please tell me it's not," Alex implored.

"My son, it is, or I would not have come to see you this evening. If these things were not true, if she is to go with you, then let it be. Her will is her own. Her future belongs to her alone. But this I must tell you, my son, with this knowledge, you can protect her and she will trust you to protect her, too. Love her if you wish to love her but remember she can never truly be yours to love. Don't destroy her happiness and your honour for a moment of pleasure unless you are willing to make the sacrifices that will be demanded of you."

"Have you told her?" Alex questioned.

The doctor remained silent.

"Why haven't you told her, why?" Alex pleaded.

"I have tried. Believe me my son, I have tried, but she will not listen. She is not ready to know and so in accordance with her wishes, I have remained silent until this day. This knowledge will be with you. Should I not survive her return, the story will be with you and you will pass this to her when the time is right. When you know the path is clear, when you see the heavens are open and the stars are shining. You will know the time is right."

10

Purple Palaces

When the invaders brutally sacked the palace grounds, an eight-year-old boy with a gold turban, dressed in a cream silk suit, stealed away from the marriage fire, desperately trying to escape the scenes of horror around him. Slithering like a snake underneath the two bridal thrones, each adorned with pure gold thread upholstery, the boy curled up into a bundle, hoping he would not be detected. Hidden behind a heavy gold frill, he buried his head in his arms and covered his ears to block the screams of terror and bullets ricocheting through the courtyard. This was the bravest thing he had ever done. The boy lay there motionless, speechless, and desperate to cry out but too afraid to make a sound. Swallowing hard several times, the lump in his throat refused to budge. He knew he could stay alive if he could just stay out of sight. But he also suspected that his family could well be dead. Trying hard to control his emotions and taking enough deep breaths to remain calm, the boy wondered how he was going to survive without them. He wanted to cry out for his mother but he couldn't find his voice. He wanted to run and put his arms around his father but he felt paralyzed from the waist down. Courageously, he found the strength to put his hands together and pray for his family, his home, and his throne. He prayed for the past, he prayed for the present, he prayed for the future he knew he might never have. As the evening came and went he stayed hidden under the ornate thrones. Now, the cries had long ago stopped. The attackers had gone. Women and children, husbands and fathers were no longer wailing. The boy was tired and hungry but he was too scared to move, so he stayed put until exhaustion overcame him and he fell asleep.

Moments before dawn, the palace grounds still shrouded in dusk, the boy woke up and pulled aside the gold frill. He could see the sun rising in the distance that seemed to him like a million miles away. The stench was unbearable and he heaved. The boy crawled out, wiping the perspiration from his forehead with his sleeve. Within moments rays of light streamed onto the palace grounds, confirming the stark reality of the murders committed the day before. The fountain sprayed cool water into the air. Centred in the courtyard it ran hellish red. Mangled bodies lay intermingled with gory snow leopard carcasses, the courtyard resembling a butcher's shop. Spent from nausea and repulsion, eyeing several menacing vultures hovering nearby, the boy tried to find his parents. Then the odour overpowered him and he heaved.

The boy found his dead parents, and wept. He was inconsolable. He cried out in pain, screaming in terror, hugging them, trying to bring them back to life. Then, clenching his fists, he was overcome with anger, unable to understand how the palace could have been discovered, and why no one had tried to stop them. The boy knew well the mystery that surrounded Malamar. It was a fairytale, a myth involving royal grounds, fast-flowing rivers and streams. His family often told him the story of the years spent camouflaging the trails with an intricate puzzle of wild overgrown mazes and gigantic conifers. He wondered if these stories were true. Even the servants had joked about it. The boy remembered his mother telling of when she would sneak down to the village of Surinsar for provisions. It suddenly occurred to the boy that he had never been to Surinsar. In fact, he realized that he had never been beyond the palace walls with the exception of the cave temples and even then he had been escorted by his mother. He had no idea what he was going to do or where he would go.

The boy walked around the courtyard until at last he found the little princess. She was alive. She was crying. The little princess had been buried under a heap of dead bodies unable to free herself. The intense morning sun finally appeared over the horizon and the bright sunlight glanced off her copper hair.

"Princess," he whispered, "is that you?" The fallen carcass of a hefty rider had crushed the eight-year-old girl to the ground. The bloodstained corpse had splattered over her and blood from his open mouth had trickled into her ear. The horror of the image made the boy vomit.

"Take my hand?" the boy whispered gently.

"I cannot, please, understand, I cannot," the little princess replied, sobbing trying to suppress her anguish.

The boy knelt down and with a strength he never thought he had, he pushed the body off the little princess. He removed his bloodstained jacket to cover her.

"Don't ... don't look at me ... don't come closer," the little princess pleaded, "I am naked."

It was at this moment the boy felt a compulsion for survival, a feeling that would never leave him. While he knew his deeply-embedded wounds would never heal, he did not want them to determine his future either. It was also the day the boy found a force so compelling it would forever forge his character and his destiny.

Years later, at the age of twenty-three, Jovi completed his first major project, The Cascades, renovating an aging hotel in Agra. His overnight success in Agra inspired him to return to the Palace of Malamar, eight hundred miles away, a place he had neglected for so many years. Jovi's idea to resurrect the damaged and dormant, yet imposing structure was a bold one. He wanted to create an atmosphere at the palace more magical even than before. Nevertheless, the project haunted him. Going back brought back memories he had long ago buried.

Despite all the odds, Jovi was eager to forge a setting so compelling it would take one's breath away. He was also determined to find a way to give the complex surrounding the palace a magical feel and he often referred to this project as The Magical Mahal. Jovi constantly thought of the Taj Mahal in Agra. *How can I preserve the old structure and rebuild a new one of the future? How can I modernize the interiors so that it could be lived in and yet design the exterior so that it would excite visitors? I want to bring the Palace of Malamar back to life again.* So, he set about to achieve his ultimate venture; the metamorphosis of the Purple Palace of Malamar.

Jovi's first undertaking was to build a road large enough to haul truckloads of granite and marble. Along the route, he built The Log Cabin Inn, a small inn next to the waterfalls. This served as his temporary residence. After months of painstaking discussions with local authorities, they finally began the construction of the Malamar road. Starting in the town of Surinsar, it stretched to the village of Sambara. The road from Surinsar to Malamar traced the old route along the river, to the waterfalls. This eventually inclined dangerously uphill to the palace grounds. The road itself had been a long and costly affair. Nonetheless, he managed to strike a lucrative deal with the local authorities. Jovi offered to pay for the road and renovate the ailing local school in exchange for sole ownership of the Malamar palace and grounds. At long last he was to own the land that was rightly his.

It was two years later, in the spring when the rebirth of the Palace of Malamar was finally completed. Jovi had spent months overseeing every minute detail before he moved in. Supervising a team of a few highly skilled engineers and architects, he had hired mostly local artisans thus boosting employment in both Surinsar and Sambara.

With the Palace of Malamar, Jovi reunited romance and pleasure, whilst creating a complex mix of old values and new ideas. Each room and every space he imbued with his own unique style. Jovi was gifted and it showed. He had the expertise, the knack, the knowledge and he used these qualities to the utmost. Finally, the meticulous and elaborate renovation of the Purple Palace of Malamar was completed.

When Jovi abruptly left Paris in Agra without a note of explanation, it had been a difficult and intuitive decision which weighed heavily on his mind and heart. Although convinced of his love, he had to be sure she was the one. But no matter how hard he tried to justify his actions in Agra, he deeply regretted charging off without so much as a note, wanting only to get back to the palace as fast as he could.

A private jet flew Jovi and his companion to Jammu. He felt uneasy and unsure. Uneasy about the way he had treated Paris, and unsure of the young woman he was with and how she would adjust to a life without him. Jovi wondered if or how his companion would be able to reintegrate into a world she had left long ago. *And Paris …?* Seeing her for the first time in Agra, he had not expected his emotions to spin out of control. Jovi and the mysterious young woman, stayed the night at the Winter Palace Hotel.

They sat together on the terrace that night. Dressed in a simple white cotton dress, the young woman asked,

"You're leaving me, Jovi, aren't you?" She was hurt. And he could not bear to hear the sadness in her voice. He didn't look up.

"Yes, only for a few days my dearest. I'll be back before the end of the week," he replied avoiding the bleak look in her eyes.

"The Palace?" she asked probingly. "Are you going back?"

"Yes," he said, flicking through a magazine. He raised an eyebrow and glanced at her fleetingly.

"When will it end Jovi, when?" the young woman pleaded, looking away. She got up and walked over to the window overlooking the Winter Palace Hotel gardens and the vista down to the lake.

"You should come with me," Jovi suggested.

The young woman took a deep breath. A few moments later, after mulling over his words, she returned to her chair.

"I can't, I'm sorry but I'm not ready!" Jovi pretended he hadn't heard her.

The young woman continued, "I say to myself that I will be brave and believe me, I think about it everyday. I say that I will go back to Malamar and that I can make that journey along the river, but in truth ... this is as far as I can go! Forgive me, Jovi, can you forgive me?"

Her cheeks flushed and tears rolled down her face. Jovi put his arms around her shoulders and this made her feel safe.

"Stay then, my darling," he said consolingly, "stay here and wait for me. I'll be back before the end of the week ... you can use the cell phone ... we won't be far from each other."

"What's she like?"

"Who?" Jovi responded, startled at her sudden brashness.

"Malamar? What's she like?"

"She's original, she's ours, she belongs to us. You should come with me. If you did you'd fall in love with her as I have."

"Next time, perhaps ... next time," the young woman said, adding with a sigh, "I love you Jovi, you're all I've got."

Jovi pulled her closer and stroked her hair, until the young woman stopped crying.

The following day, before dusk, Jovi arrived at The Log Cabin Inn. Without a moment to lose, before dark, he changed into waterproofs and crossed the nearby ravine on foot. The distant crashing of the waterfall was clearly audible as he waded through knee-high water for a good ten minutes. Eventually, Jovi came upon the tiny inlet he had discovered, quite by accident while excavating the route to Malamar two years before. He searched for more clues, but to his disappointment, there was still nothing other than eerie echoes of constant dripping water. There he remembered how he had discovered a tattered golden organza shawl. Jovi remembered it well, knowing whom it belonged to. When he held the crumpled, bloodstained shawl in his hands, the dirt disintegrated in his fingers like henna drying from a bride's delicate hands. Jovi had taken it back to the inn where he had carefully soaked it in warm water, until the dirt had washed away.

Jovi reflected back to the day the palace had become a bloodbath. *What must it have been like for the little princess as she roamed the forest alone,* he wondered? *How she must have suffered, how she must have endured, not only unbearable agony but also unimaginable despair.* Jovi began to imagine that day, years ago, how she must have fought for her life. Many times he had returned to the inlet hoping to find more clues that the little princess was still alive.

To gaze is to think and that was exactly what Jaleena was doing. Sitting alone in the Winter Palace Hotel, gazing into thin air, she knew that eventually she would have to make a decision. A decision of a lifetime, and one she had been avoiding all her adult life.

Jovi had been her saviour. Without him, Jaleena would never have survived. He had saved her life, rescued her from horror and freed her from the shadow of despair that had tormented her since the day she had been crushed under the chest of her would-be assassin. Jaleena's recovery had been long and arduous.

When finally her nurses advised Jovi, that Jaleena would be better taken care of in Europe, he quickly transferred her to a convalescent home in Switzerland. Shortly afterward, Jovi also moved to Switzerland where he completed his education at a school located in a ski resort in the Alps. When Jaleena recovered she completed her schooling and graduated as a translator from Geneva University. At about the time she found a job at the United Nations in Geneva, Jovi graduated, at twenty-one, from the renowned Le Corbusier School of Architecture for Digital Design, in Montreux. Shortly, thereafter, Jovi set up his own company, Dream Machines.

Lost in thought, Jaleena realised how much she loved him. Jovi's support had been genuine. *Why had she never seen him with a woman? Why had he never fallen in love? Had she been an obstacle in his life*, she worried. *Could she be the reason why he would never love*, she speculated with pangs of guilt. *But maybe this was to change*, she thought, when she saw Jovi's interest in a photo magazine in Switzerland. *It was the way he had looked at the photos*, Jaleena pondered, *as well as the sudden rearrangement of our flight home. His eagerness to go to Agra had been most unusual, his mood distinctly out of character. And then there was the beautiful woman at The Abbey*, she ruminated. *Who was she?*

Now, Jaleena thought, *they were back at the Winter Palace Hotel.* Jovi had given her no convincing explanation concerning his sudden departure to the Palace of Malamar. Jovi's desire to take her with him had been more than alarming to Jaleena. *As the transformation of the palace neared completion,* she mused, *he did nothing but talk about it. He had been ecstatic and overwhelmed with excitement but never before had he dared ask me to go there.*

Moreover, there was the matter of Jaleena's own life, so closely linked to Jovi's. She depended on him. *Could this be the reason why he let no other woman in his life?* These thoughts raced around in her mind as no other man, had come along who'd lived up to her expectations. Realizing she was searching for Jovi's rare qualities, she wondered whether she had depended on him too much for her own good. Jaleena made her decision. She arranged for a car to drive her to Sambara. She called Jovi to let him know, but his cell phone was switched off. Jaleena called the Quarters Hotel announcing her arrival.

Sutton's phone call to Paris at The Cascades arrived minutes after she had received his fax.

"Paris, I know of no words of condolence can bring your father back. If it's any consolation at all, I want you to know you're not alone." Sutton was desperate to find words to console her and for the first time since he'd known her, he felt powerless, almost weak. The tragic news was seriously affecting his ability to deal with this death, any death.

"Sutton, I can't even express how empty I feel right now," Paris sobbed, grateful to hear his comforting voice.

"Even though I didn't know him personally, I know how close you two were. I know he was a courageous man ... a true inspiration for all of us! He loved you so very much!"

"You know Sutton, I never imagined this would ever happen. I never prepared myself for this. If only I hadn't stopped in Agra I would have been home for him."

"No one can see into the future and you can't punish yourself for not being there. I spoke to Seetha," Sutton said gently. "She told me Keta died peacefully ... in his sleep. She told me to tell you, he didn't suffer. She's waiting for you to come home."

"He was a strong man, Sutton. He was a man with such ... goals, such ... such a ... sense ... of ... pride ... and ... great determination!"

Alone at The Cascades in Agra, grief-stricken and anxious to leave, Paris felt guilty, guilty for thinking so much about Jovi and guilty for not being able to grieve for her father completely, the way he deserved. Her heart was split into so many bits and pieces that each and every emotion hurt. The pain of passion for Jovi, the pain of grief for her father, and the pain of losing Alex, upset her. Paris tried to close her mind to Alex and keep her feelings from Jovi, but no matter how hard she tried, she could not help thinking about them.

Paris's journey from Agra to Sambara was troublesome. Having tried desperately to arrange a flight leaving immediately, she had to stay at The Cascades for yet another night. Although flights leaving Agra were almost completely booked, she finally managed to get herself on an early morning flight to New Delhi, the next day, connecting to Jammu. When she finally landed and was on the road home, she felt somewhat relieved. It wasn't until she finally arrived at the clinic and read the letter her father had left for her that she let herself grieve openly for him. When she had received the news announcing her father's sudden death days earlier she could only feel empty.

It was an odd day, she would remember years later, the day she discovered her father had left her a farewell letter, knowing he was dying. Her father had planned his life, and now in death he had planned her destiny. Paris would often reflect that he had been a man of great strength, a believer in the impossible, devout in his prayers and solid in his judgments. His love, she would often muse, had moulded her life and given her a willpower that would be with her forever.

My dearest Angel,

I remember when you were young, when you used to play at the Saraswati Temple on the banks of a stream in Sambara. Marigolds, ah yes, I remember how you loved the scent of marigolds. I further remember I knew little English in those days, learned only from discarded books I found on many of my journeys. Of course, those were the most cherished days of your childhood. These are memories of happy times and sweet recollections. Now, I have the capacity to communicate fully in English and in depth, but that innocent childhood has left you!

Today is Sunday and your mother and I sit together thinking of you. Our thoughts of you are as fresh as springtime. Your words are as sweet as our rivers. Your youth is the Himalayan blossoms plucked from the orange and apricot trees. It gives us much happiness to remember you and your unique ways.

When I brought you home you became our devoted daughter and my inspiration. You were my goal, my aim, my vision of loveliness and my hopes for goodness. When I gave you my heart, you became my treasured jewel. This warm feeling I have cherished from the first day.

On lonely nights, sitting close to the log fire with your mother, I would think of you, my daughter. When you left, I could not be consoled. I sensed your presence. I felt the air currents when you would whirl by. I knew you well. I can only admire you for your courage to go and live your creative, prosperous life. I shall explore the world, you said with admirable conviction. I never forgot your excitement and your earnest words.

Today I write to you with a heavy heart and news more painful. Do you remember when I found you in the forest? Well on that day, I took an oath to protect you until you were ready to hear the truth about your lost heritage. These last months I recalled this story many times.

I found you near Malamar, along the shores of the river. Travelling alone through the deep forest, leaving you safely with my mules, I climbed up to the giant conifers when I saw the pillars of a palace. I had discovered the lost world of Malamar. Its allure was so dazzling that it momentarily blinded me. An overpowering, eerie silence frightened me and at first I was afraid to pass through the mythical gates guarded by two pink elephants.

It is with sadness that I must reveal to you, my tender-hearted daughter, that your entire family was brutally murdered years ago. I found you fleeing from the terror. Your courageous mother survived for a short time after the attackers left. She gave me her ruby necklace as proof of your heritage, as a symbol of your legacy, and finally as a token of her love.

Your ancestry is very noble and you are the sole survivor of the royal family of the Palace of Malamar. This place you will find in the heart of the Himalayas, beyond the Surinsar wall. It is the land of the rare snow leopards. It is a land of exotic beauty. It is a garden, a paradise for angels to fall to earth to play and enchant us mortal humans. You are, my dearest daughter, Princess Parisa of this ancient kingdom.

Your mother believes you somehow remember. Telling you openly she thinks may hurt you. Now as I write, I see your mother is wise. You never spoke of your past. You never burdened us, on the contrary, you showered us with your affection.

I gave you a gold box. Inside is the necklace. This is proof of your identity, evidence of your royal heritage. This will be worn when your heart is ready.

If you have this letter in your possession then I have passed into another world. Let me assure you that this enchanting world is as glorious as the majestic mountain peaks of Surinsar. It is the place where my memories of you will be celebrated to the sweet melody of the angelic harp. It is a world where my spirit will finally rest in peace.

I wish only for my ashes to be scattered in the ravine by the waterfalls where I found you. You must go alone. From there, my child, I insist, you must trace the path back to the palace. This is my wish, my only wish, my beloved child, my gracious daughter. I will watch over you from the heavens. You will never be alone.

Your loving father.

The next day, driving alone, Paris passed by Lake Surinsar and joined the inclining road up to Malamar. Hardly able to recognize the new road leading into the forest, Paris's thoughts drifted. Visions of her father came back into her mind, as well as images of the cave temples which had until now remained souvenirs of the past. As she plodded uphill in the car, deep into the forest, clumps of yellow cinquefoils rimmed the route. *The fierce wilderness*, Paris thought.

Paris came to an abrupt halt outside The Log Cabin Inn, built from pine logs and covered in shiny green ivy. It looked as if it had come straight from the pages of a children's fairytale. In the distance, she could hear the sound of water smashing down onto rocks. Paris felt this must be the waterfalls her father had mentioned in his letter. She jumped out of the car and made her way toward the waterfalls. Suddenly the scenery around her, which had been buried in her memory for so many years, became startlingly familiar and she began to recall precise events from years ago. Paris took a deep breath and looked at the surroundings with new eyes.

As the falls came into view, a group of dancing yellow butterflies fluttered on and off the water. Paris plucked a few touch-me-not flowers, their fragrance bursting into the mountain air. Pine trees, oak trees, walnut trees and larch conifers towered over the cliff as she approached the water. Paris spotted several monkeys ogling overhead in a dhak tree full of red blooms. The wind whirled as she paid her last respects and scattered her father's ashes near the waterfalls. Words of sorrow, words of grief, words of comfort and words of wisdom, poured out from Paris's heart. Remembering her father's devotion to the ancient works of the Vedas, she recited these verses from the book of Atharva Veda.

We are the birds of the same nest
We may wear different skins
We may speak in different tongues
We may believe in different religions
We may belong to different cultures
Yet we share the same home,
Our Earth

Born on the same planet
Covered by the same skies
Gazing at the same stars
Breathing the same air,
We must learn to happily progress together
Or miserably perish together
For we can live individually
But can only survive collectively

In lingering early morning gloom, Alex gathered his belongings and feeling sentimental, set out for the Quarters Hotel. Driving alone, he arrived at the new road leading to the village. Longing for Mr. Patel with his elongated moustache, he remembered his long lost companion's dry sense of humour, as well as the hair-raising hairpin bends they drove through together.

The car chugged uphill to the outskirts of the village. Dawn burst over the distant horizon, followed by the rising sun. As it peeped beyond the rugged snow range of the Surinsar wall, he slammed on the brakes, grabbed his camera and snapped as many pictures as he could. Totally immersed, he realized for the first time, since Paris had left him, he felt calm and relaxed. The gloomy feeling of late, had disappeared. Every click of the camera drew him closer to Paris, opening his heart, making him feel worthy of her. *Perhaps this will be my lucky day after all*, he thought. *Something out there was waiting for him, and someone out there was about to change his life*, Alex reflected.

Alex drove directly to the clinic in anticipation. It was shut, but the sign, to his surprise, was still there. He continued onto the Quarters Hotel and to his delight, it had been tastefully renovated. The original style and its cosy ambience had not changed, but the creaking wooden steps had been replaced. It was only after he had checked in, he heard about the death of the village doctor and the arrival of his daughter who had scattered her father's ashes at the waterfalls the previous day.

After scattering her father's ashes, Paris spent the night at the inn. She slept soundly, waking to a hazy morning. Paris prepared to hike to the palace before lunch.

Jaleena packed her suitcase at the Winter Palace Hotel. She called Jovi again on his cell phone but there was still no response.

II

The Heart of Paris

*A*s Alex approached the inn that morning, the mist hovered persistently, although the sun tried its best to emerge through elusive rain clouds. As he screeched to a halt outside, a small gathering of curious monkeys bounced on the roof of his car. Shooing them off, he grabbed his camera bag and headed to the front porch.

Early the same morning Paris dressed quickly in loose-fitting black jeans and hiking shoes. Comfortable and warm in a large cream polo neck sweater and a blue mackintosh she prepared to hike to the palace via a trail through the woods. The imposing mist outdoors did not deter her as she headed for the front door.

Alex's mind was spinning in anticipation. Soon he would be able to speak his mind, hold Paris in his arms and tell her how much he loved her. Remembering St. Moritz filled him with terrible remorse. Loving her gave him hope. Losing her filled him with apprehension. Finding her and holding her close, excited him beyond anything he had known before. Alex's heart pounded ever faster as his emotions whirled in suspenseful expectation.

Before she left the inn, Paris peered out the window and noticed a curtain of yellow butterflies flitting by and then grief for her father overwhelmed her again. Her eyes clouded with tears. Paris then reflected on her imprudence of the last few days. How could Jovi deceive her, how could he have tricked her into believing that he loved her and how could she have fallen so completely in love with him? And there was the matter concerning Alex. Was he not heading into treacherous territory as her half-hearted lover? *What is love then?* she asked herself. *Who is Jovi? Why is love so wicked and unbearable, so heavenly and so full of sadness?* Images of Jovi flooded into her thoughts while dark shadows of the mysterious woman in his life chilled her to the bone. Loving two extraordinary men at the same time filled her with confusion.

Paris opened the door with a heavy heart, a mass of rain clouds floated overhead. Intense rays of sunlight beamed into her eyes, blurring her vision. As she turned, Paris caught sight of a familiar face.

"Alex, what on earth are you doing here? How on earth did you find me?" she asked aghast.

"I knew you'd be here. I heard about your father at the Quarters Hotel and I'm so so sorry. I just followed you here."

Alex, overwhelmed with desire, almost buckled at the knees. With tremendous restraint, he spoke in an even tone he had been practicing for days, trying to say the words every way but backwards.

"I love you," he said, as he looked earnestly into her alluring dark eyes.

Paris, unable to endure such intensity lashed back angrily.

"For heaven's sake, Alex, how can you tell me that now! You hardly dared to kiss me, let alone anything else. You've been so aloof, so distant. You acted as if you didn't care about me … about us!" she said bursting into tears.

"Listen Paris … I do care about you! You take my breath away! You enrapture me! You're the most ravishing, captivat-

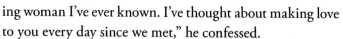

ing woman I've ever known. I've thought about making love to you every day since we met," he confessed.

Paris seized her chance. "So at least you thought about it … just never bothered to tell me you're in love with me!"

"Darn it … I couldn't do it … I couldn't do it!" he said fiercely banging his fist against the front door.

"Why?" She yelled, lifting her dignified head.

"Because I made a promise."

"To whom?" she barked furiously, fighting back the tears.

"To your father … to Keta … Come on, Paris, you've known who you are, all your life, you just never wanted to admit it. You see, that's why I couldn't make love to you. I couldn't love you as I wanted to. Darn it … I had to hold back. I knew you were mad at me in St. Moritz. You were mad at me for not making love to you … and for trying to convince myself I wasn't in love with you, then telling you that I didn't love you. But you knew it wasn't true! You said so in your poem."

"For heaven's sake Alex, what on earth did you promise my father?" Paris pounded back.

"I promised … promised … I would never *never* make love to you just for the sake of the moment. You see … you were never mine to have and your father made that clear to me the night before I left Sambara."

"Oh my God … what did he say?" she asked, her courage faltering.

"*He said … he said … you're mar … you're mar …*"

"I'm what, for heaven's sake Alex, what are you trying to say?"

"He said you are *mar ...*" and then suddenly he realized she had no idea what he was talking about. Paris knew nothing about the ceremonial wedding that had taken place years ago. Changing his mind rapidly, Alex decided that he could not tell her. Paris would be lost to him forever.

"Marvellous! You're marvellous! Damn it ... you're marvellous and then he told me details ... and more details ... as if I wanted to hear more detail." He continued dispiritedly, "All about myths and legends, Malamar and you, your past, your destiny ... which ... by the way ... I'm not part of. Look, damn it ... if I'm an honourable man, a man who keeps his word, then what I didn't do or say was out of respect for your father and you! These were my reasons. Paris, believe me, if a man could give you more love, I would step aside ... reluctantly ... no ... darn it ... I'd never step aside!"

"Do you really love me Alex?"

"Believe me, Paris, I've always loved you!" he said with conviction.

Paris, determined not to let him off so easily, held firm.

"Honestly Alex, why didn't you tell me? I also have feelings ... also have a heart ... I also feel love and passion just as much as you. You should have told me you loved me years ago," she said desperately, wiping back tears. "Why are you here?" Paris asked, stunned.

"Because after you left I couldn't imagine life without you."

Wiping her eyes, trying to find her handkerchief, Paris stumbled away from him. After a moment of painful silence, she turned to look deeply into his sea-green eyes and realized how much he must have suffered. A pang of deep loss

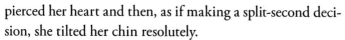

pierced her heart and then, as if making a split-second decision, she tilted her chin resolutely.

"I'm going to find the palace."

He dove in trying to prevent her from slipping away.

"You shouldn't go alone … I've a car, let me drive you."

"No thanks, Alex."

At wit's end, he implored, "Damn it, Paris, do you have to go?"

"Yes, this is the moment I've been waiting a long time for … finding enough courage to come to terms with my past … look … I'll be back in the morning."

"You're crazy going all that way in weather like this, let me take you, it's too dangerous … you haven't been back here in years and …," his voice trailed off in disappointment.

"Believe me, Alex, I've done this kind of thing before … I'm not a kid, I'll be fine." Then, as if she were under a terrific strain, "I've met someone else," she said, deliberately breaking his heart.

Alex, imagining her tawny body in someone else's arms, looked at her in horror.

Bleary-eyed and weary, she went on, "I've met him somewhere before, but I don't know where. I can't place him … I just know he means a lot to me."

Alex's mood changed as the unbearable torment of rejection numbed his senses. He swayed backward and gripped the edge of the door. Blood drained from his already pale face.

"Paris," he said unable to contain his passion for her, "I've come here to ask you to marry me. Will you marry me, my darling, will you marry me, my love?"

As the words spilled, he felt his honour slip away, as well as the promises he had made to her father two years ago.

12

Reaching for Paradise

$\mathcal{P}$aris trekked through the mist following an old and unfamiliar trail. She ploughed on through dusky pink heather until she came to the path leading to a group of towering conifers. From there, Paris discovered an entangled labyrinth and a cluster of bo trees. The flow of the river rushed into view. It was only then that Paris spotted the looming marble pillars of the palace.

Stunned, her mind raced back to her past. Faint images of her father's miraculous presence appeared, his warm hands feeding her drops of honey. Paris began to sense her connection to this place, to the great and bygone dynasties. As she took in their sheer magnificence, she saw the pillars change colour from lavender to mauve, from mauve to blue and then shades of fading blues. Paris suddenly felt tense as she followed the uphill trail until the pillars bizarrely disappeared from view. She lingered for a while, wondering which way to go. Delving deeply into her memory, she recalled that the Palace of Malamar sat north of the rising sun, so she took the path pointing in that direction. Perplexing memories of a wild stray snow leopard roaming in the woods increased her tension. These recurring memories sent shivers down her spine, as she vividly recalled plunging to freedom, clinging onto a golden organza shawl. Casting her mind back to how she stole away on a blanket of gravely dirt only to be rescued by her father, the dearest man of her young life, caused her to break down and cry uncontrollably.

Paris trekked on, until she came across a maze of shrubs obstructing her path. She cleared it, whereupon she recognized a gigantic banyan tree buried so deeply in her the back of her mind. *So it was real,* she thought, *it was true - the snow leopards, the cocoon, the shawl, the honey salve, the waterfalls, the inlet and … the wedding. Was that true, too,* she wondered, fearing the answer. Instinctively she looked into the skies for the vultures, remembering how they had scoffed and soared above her tiny body.

As the banyan trees fell behind, the palace came into sight. It towered in the heavens in all its majestic glory. Two bejewelled pink elephants flanked the entrance. Paris looked on in astonishment, disbelieving the full extent of its grandeur. The striking salmon-pink bodies, dressed up in ceremonial costume placed strategically at the end of several vast green manicured lawns, impressed her. Hundreds of yellow cinquefoils rimmed the path to the entrance. Paris ran to the elephants whose trunks soared in the air. Tall lanky pine trees dotted the lawns. Smaller ornamental ones had been expertly pruned into coils representing the three-dimensions of the palace, better known as the helix, the crest of the palace. Paris investigated further.

Dark clouds covered the sky. The breeze chilled and the slender pine trees swayed in the wind. The gates burst open to a horse rider heading for the woods, furiously galloping out of the palace grounds into the wind. The gates began to close. Paris hurtled herself through the opening barrier before they shut behind her.

Paris, tall and sultry, her hair flowing and sparkling, entered. The old courtyard had been transformed into a vast garden. The gardens were blooming with hundreds of purple irises, white miniature roses and sweet williams. Several arches, covered with sweet pea intermingling with lavender wisteria, and rambling wild pink roses led the way to large iron gates. The gates were intricately decorated with elaborate lotus flowers, colourful peacocks, flamboyant parrots and baroque blooming red roses. The long and narrow path was lined with lights. Paris continued, almost in a trance, unable to believe that she was witnessing the re-birth of the Palace of Malamar.

Paris saw a cluster of dark grey clouds open up to dispel huge quantities of rain. Thunder roared overhead with several flashes of lightning. The dry air became denser and warmer. Paris headed for the main residence barely recognizing anything at all. The palace was deserted. The huge oak door was wide open. She tiptoed inside and up the stairs. Recognizing her old bedroom, she looked inside. A large oak wardrobe stood in one corner, there were Tiffany lamps on tables either side of an ancient four-poster bed which had hundreds of fresh red rose petals scattered over it. Then, Paris noticed the door to the oak wardrobe was ajar. Inside she discovered a saffron silk sari embroidered with silver roses. Finding it irresistible she slipped it on.

Paris was astonished to find a diamond necklace and matching earrings on top of a red velvet box lying on the dressing table. She slipped on several silver bangles and pinned her hair into a chignon. Distracted by a horse trotting outside, she peered out the window to see the return of the mysterious rider. A black shiny horse with a wild and rapturous mane swaggered under threatening thunderclouds. As wisps of scattered rain started to trickle, Paris left the room.

A tall dark man wearing fitted black jeans and an unbuttoned white shirt, dismounted. He removed his leather riding gloves, brushed aside his dishevelled hair and stroked his horse affectionately. Bashful Beauty snuggled up and nuzzled against her master's jet-black hair. Stupefied by the silhouette of a tall and svelte woman approaching, he held his breath and raised his eyebrows in surprise.

"Paris?" he called out incredulously.

"Jovi, what are you doing here?" she asked, bewildered.

"I live here … this is my home!" he said proudly.

"It can't be, it's mine … I mean … it used to be … who are you … why are you following me?" she bellowed back, as thunder blasted in the distance. His shirt clung to his body. Paris felt a maddening and irresistible urge to bolt into his arms. A fierce gust wind unravelled her chignon, blowing it around her shoulders. Lightning struck again in the far distance and trickles of rain began to fall. Paris, framed in this way, her damp saffron sari clinging to her, looked ravishing to him. At a loss for words, he shuddered.

Paris wondered how many more surprises were in store. *First Alex and now this*, she thought. "For heaven's sake, I can't take anymore!" she groaned through the flurry of rain, "Who are you?"

"Jovi of Malamar and you are Princess Parisa," he replied in a deep soothing voice.

Staggering forward, she began to sob. Jovi rushed over to block her fall and envelop her in his strong arms. Paris was shivering with fear, shivering with emotion, shivering with the knowledge that the truth had finally been revealed. Their lips brushed softly as tears for so many reasons trickled down her olive skin. Jovi folded her more closely into his powerful hold and lavished her neck and shoulders with small kisses.

"I love you Paris ... you've found your own way home and I love you for this as I love you for everything you are ... so please don't get upset ... this should be the happiest day of your life."

"But you knew all this the whole time I was with you in Agra? Why didn't you tell me who you really are and who I am?" she demanded.

When I saw you at The Cascades I recognized you but I wasn't sure until you wore the ruby necklace."

"How did you find me?"

"*Cyber* magazine! The special supplement on Paris Cassidis ... remember, a Portrait of Paris? You are the image of your mother and her portrait hangs in the main hall of the palace ... that's how."

"But that doesn't explain the necklace?"

"The necklace is a family heirloom. I don't know how you got it."

She cast her mind back to her father's letter. *It was mostly all there, the explanation, the truth, the reality ... there in the letter.*

"You should have told me the truth at The Cascades," she said, agonizing while still locked in his embrace.

"I wanted you to love me for myself ... not ... for Malamar, not for The Cascades!" Jovi said as his hands tightened around her waist.

"What's that got to do with it or Malamar for that matter?" she snapped, pulling away. Jovi refused to let her go and pulled her back firmly.

"I own it."

"And so what difference does it make?" Paris asked falling desperately in love and noticing how pale Jovi looked. She felt deeply touched. *He never gave up searching*, she reflected, *he never gave up believing. Jovi never gave up on me.*

"I know it wouldn't have made a difference to you at all. I restored the hotel and renamed it The Cascades, dedicating it to you after I found your shawl in an inlet behind the waterfalls."

"What?" she said aghast, ashamed of doubting him.

"Well, that's how I figured you were still alive ... that somehow you had not witnessed the massacre at the Palace of Malamar. You could never sit still, always running around and playing. I prayed for your safety ... I prayed that you'd done what you always used to do and that was to run off to play. When the murderers left, I came looking for you."

"I went to play hide and seek. I was only six," she muttered, pleading forgiveness under her breath as she turned ghostly pale.

"I know ... I knew in my heart that you were still alive ... that they hadn't murdered you as they did the others."

"But you've betrayed me Jovi, you have another woman?" she protested bitterly, removing his grip.

"What are you talking about?" he said roughly, moving away.

"I saw you with another woman at The Cascades. She was pretty and terribly in love with you." Terrified of this truth, Paris began to sob. Jovi cupped her face, bringing it close to his and then enveloped her in his arms again.

"No, Paris, listen to me ... stop crying and listen ... she's Jaleena, my twin sister!"

Rain started to pelt down. At that inopportune moment, another swollen cloud burst open. Paris slipped through Jovi's arms and buckled to the ground. He carried her inside, out of the driving rain, and draped her onto a chintz divan. *Nothing,* he thought, *could disguise the long legs, the long dark eyelashes and the voluptuous swell of her breasts under her damp saffron sari.* As her anguished eyes fluttered open, Jovi knelt by her side holding her hand.

"Listen … they brutally murdered everyone leaving no witnesses except for myself and Jaleena."

"Oh my god, our parents, our families, my governess … they must have suffered so much," Paris said as tears flooded her eyes.

"Yes, they suffered. It was horrible."

"How did you escape Jovi … how?"

"I hid under the thrones. I was small enough to hide under them and no one bothered to look for me there."

"And Jaleena, what happened to her?"

"Look Paris, they tried to rape her but she struggled. She's brave and courageous. Jaleena managed to slay her assassin by stabbing him in the neck with his own dagger. He fell on top of her and crushed her to the ground. She stayed buried and blood-soaked all through the night."

"Oh no … oh my God … no … how horrible!"

"You know, Paris, Jaleena has the strength to put up with anything but that was too much for her, it was too gross, too cruel and she still suffers. When I found her the following morning, she was completely naked and trapped. If they'd discovered her, they'd have mutilated her like the others that day."

"Oh Jovi, I'm so sorry!" she cried as she gripped him more tightly.

"Who did this, who were they, why did they do what they did?" Paris asked, exploding into tears again.

"Look, I've been trying to piece the puzzle myself for many years but I believe they were deserters who became renegade hunters and then … murderers."

"But why?"

"Well, during that time, it was common to kill snow leopards for food. In my view, these half-starved soldiers deployed on the line of control were so poorly paid that when they realized how precious the animal furs were, they deserted the army. That's when they started to slaughter the leopards for big game money."

"But how did they find us? Weren't we safe from the outside world - and why the brutality toward us?"

"We thought we were safe but no one is ever safe really. Greed can turn into other things - looting, murder, abduction, rape - and it's all for money."

"If only we could turn the clock back." Paris muttered to herself, "I was afraid when I heard the noises … I hid in a banyan tree and then I ran for my life deep into the woods and fell near the waterfalls. It's a long story."

Jovi continued to explain, "When I was sure you were not there Jaleena and I fled into the forest to Surinsar. There we came across a farmer who took us in. After a while, and through discreet inquiries, a kind and well-to-do couple was found who raised us until we were old enough to fend for ourselves. Jaleena has suffered from depression since and spent many years in a clinic in Switzerland. The scars will never heal and her nightmares still persist. She's the one who was with me at The Abbey. She's the one you saw at The Cascades."

"I'm so sorry … I didn't know," said Paris tearfully.

"It's all over now ... it was a long time ago. I never thought I'd ever find you again and to think that you have been in Sambara nearly all your life and I never knew it." Jovi replied trying desperately to comfort her.

"So now I understand why you gave me the Mirabai suite, my mother's name ... it wasn't a coincidence, was it?"

"No, I had to see your reaction Paris ... but I was almost sure who you were when I saw you at The Cascades. The coincidence of the whole saga is that you reserved a room at The Cascades!"

"Destiny?" Paris suggested, pulling him closer. Half-closing her eyes she showered him with tender kisses.

"Yes, my Princess Parisa, destiny, fate, call it what you will," Jovi said, returning every kiss.

"And the marriage? Are we still married?"

"No, I don't think so ... even then the marriage would not have been considered legal."

"So why did they do it, why?" Paris implored.

"Traditions. You know. Traditions and the fear of forgetting, neglecting old and ancient customs particularly the customs of our princely states."

"So we are not married?" Paris waited for confirmation.

"No, not in the eyes of the law ... no, we are not!"

Suspenseful silence was followed by a warm glow on Jovi's face. His eyes deep with emotion began to change from blue to aquamarine and then turquoise. Jovi took a deep breath.

"Will you marry me Princess Parisa, officially, unofficially, or any way you want?"

13

Himalayan Landslide

*D*rama, for Alex, was to scale the foreboding heights of the Himalayas and to gaze outward from the highest point of the planet. He had always assumed, with staunch conviction that these daunting and challenging feats were to be the greatest moments of his life. Now, he was to be proved wrong as the agony and suspense of his intimate conversation with Paris was out in the open. *Do you love me? Have you betrayed me? Will you marry me?* The answers to those questions made his heart soar and sink. They were to leave lasting scars.

Alex stood on the porch in shock, drowning in his own silence. With so much whirling around inside his mind, he grabbed his anorak and hauled himself into his jeep. *What had I expected*, he wondered? *Has she betrayed me? Was she ever mine to betray?* For the first time Alex saw the truth clearly. *All in all, she had been honest.* He banged his fist furiously against the steering wheel, shouted her name, cried out at Paris in utter despair. Realizing she didn't want to be followed, Alex shot down the valley in his jeep, lost in thought. Then, creeping at a snail's pace along the treacherous winding bends, he glared out onto the dusty road thinking about Paris. Alex tried to imagine her loving someone else. *Paris possessed immeasurable devotion*, Alex thought. *It was hard to imagine her in another world giving her all. It was hard to imagine his world without her.*

Passing the lake of Surinsar Alex carried onto Sambara. The clouds advanced like lumbering elephants, enormous and full of rain. Along the uphill climb to the Quarters Hotel, he petered to a standstill scouring the dark clouds marching forward over the lofty range of the Surinsar wall. Alex rolled down his window to get a better look. The breeze quickened. In the distance, a gale was about to pick up speed. Then came the rains, gently at first, with a few showers and followed by thunder. Alex made a quick calculation and toyed with the idea of heading back to the inn, when lightning sparked. With a deep sense of urgency, he drove on. Alex had heard stories about the dangers of being trapped in a torrential rainstorm but had never expected to be caught up in one. *Not now,* he told himself, *not today when everything else in his life was going wrong.* At that moment, a bolt of lightning hit a nearby tree, falling in his path, Alex slammed on the brakes to avoid it. Thankfully in time, his jeep came to a stop. Alex stunned, paused for a moment. Peering through the fogged windscreen, he saw a way forward around the fallen tree. At first the jeep stalled, and then the engine came to life again. Alex drove on, feeling lucky to be alive.

The earth moved. The ground underneath his jeep shifted and catapulted the vehicle into the air. Miraculously it landed upright. Slumped on the seat and shaken, Alex desperately throttled several times until at last the engine started. He headed down the road desperately trying to beat the inevitable ... a Himalayan landslide!

The back tyres burst, Alex slammed on the brakes and the vehicle swerved on the slippery surface, ploughing to a halt. Desperate, Alex had no alternative but to abandon his car. Slinging his cameras over his shoulder, he charged down the road, fighting against the deluge of rain beating against his body. There was a huge roar followed by a tumultuous collision, he glanced over his shoulder to see the complete devastation of his jeep. The shattered roof was all that remained as the rest of it had been swallowed up by the earth as the road caved in around it. Alex tripped and plunged into a ravine.

Alex raises his hand to his face to block the sunlight. Someone draws the curtain shut. The room, silent and empty shadowed in the dark transforms into a moonlit lake near a castle. The first soft magical chords of Tchaikovsky's "Swan Lake" begin to play. Swans set the tone with a haunting woodwind tune. They serenely glide across the surface of the glistening lake, their brilliant white plumage flutter and spread. A young woman tall and slender, her delicate hands the colour of porcelain appears before him. Her long, thick black hair flows past her knees. Alex smiles broadly at her. She stands gracefully before him, her white chiffon sari elaborately draped around her silhouette. The transparent fabric studded with diamonds and hemmed with intricate gold motifs glitter in the moonlight. Alex feels a warm glow of expectation. Her hips are swaying slowly and her eyelids are lowered like a forlorn swan princess. Seeming never to raise them, she beckons to him. He tries to move but he feels cemented to the ground.

While the rich ascending notes of the violins play the familiar tune, he remembers his childhood, the fairytale castle, grand and palatial high on the hill. Remembering being so full of purpose then, he wonders whether his life had been worthwhile. The diamond-studded white sash of her chiffon sari delicately swished over her bare left shoulder now gently spills to the ground revealing her naked to the hips. She lifts her head and smiles, her almond eyes now wide-open and so penetrating. Alex thinks he can hear her heart beating steadily, sees her ample breasts swaying gently. He imagines spooning warm sweet Cointreau over her nipples. He imagines devouring her, licking the sweet moisture off her skin. He lies naked on the bed, his mouth watering ready to savour her. Alex closes his eyes and groans softly. Her eyelids lower revealing her dark eyelashes. As she twists her shoulders as if to loosen the rest of her diamond studded sari, his whole body burns with desire. Her nails, he notices are the colour of snow and she is holding a silver brush. With soft gentle strokes, she begins to brush her hair until it glows radiantly, every strand resembling fine silk thread. She pins a tiara studded with diamonds to her hair while the violins play a symphony of striking notes. She becomes an imperious Swan Queen. And then swooping her arms into the air, she reaches for his hand. Their mouths touch softly. Alex feels giddy, light-headed, as if he cannot breathe. The orchestra, triumphant again, plays that familiar tune.

"Radio Kashmir April 6th -- The sudden downpour last night of torrential rainstorms hit the princely state of Malamar leaving some streets in Sambara inundated and impassable. Several people died when they were swept away by floods. Homes collapsed ..."

Alex, opened his eyes, he blinked several times until the blur dissipated and then groaned in pain as he turned onto his side. He made out some voices coupled with the aroma of steamed rice and the lingering odour of fresh spices. He tried to get up but his body ached. Alex felt his head and ripped off a blood-stained bandage. He spotted his muddy jacket on the chair beside him and reaching out for it, he passed out.

Jaleena set out for the Quarters Hotel in the company of the hotel driver, Mr. Patel. At teatime, they stopped at a village to stroll through the bazaar. Leaving the car to a small gathering of ragged children skipping around it, she roamed for a while through the alleys streaming with villagers, thinking about Jovi and the Palace of Malamar. While the school buses came and went and babies slept on their mother's laps, she felt as if something good was going to happen. *How long had it been since she felt so full of optimism*, she thought. The air warmed and the earth stilled and drops of rain began to fall. Noticing the dark sinister clouds hovering overhead, she decided to return to the car. As trickles of rain fell, Mr. Patel, who had been drinking sweet tea, was already moving toward the car.

Chased by the storm they reached the Quarters Hotel. Candles were lit. Fireplaces hissed and crackled as logs burned while giant kerosene stoves in the kitchens were ignited, allowing the cooks to go about their business of preparing the evening meal. Jaleena was eating dinner, when a man burst into the hotel. He told a story of someone on the road, hurt and in need of help. Mr. Patel and the man left immediately. Jaleena was left wondering what the commotion was all about. Jaleena sat by the fire and decided to wait for Mr. Patel's return.

Upon Mr. Patel's return, Jaleena caught sight of the foreigner; she was taken by his thick locks of gold hair, broad shoulders and toned body. The sight of him lying helplessly awakened her senses; it roused her compassion and stirred her heart. *Could a man be more handsome than he is,* she thought?

Early the next morning the hotel bustled with news of the dramatic survival of a foreigner. According to hearsay, he had been a victim of the devastating landslide but had miraculously landed on the doorstep of a local farmer who, at the time, had been rounding up his herd. Half-conscious and lightly bruised, the foreigner was rushed to the Quarters Hotel in the back of Mr. Patel's car.

Jaleena, was intrigued and wanted to know more about the foreigner. When she asked Mr. Patel about him, Mr. Patel simply bowed, clasped his hands together, nodded his head in all directions and then fiddled with his elongated moustache, not saying a word.

When Alex finally came to, he lay staring at the ceiling, trying to collect his thoughts, wondering what had happened. Much to his surprise he felt a huge surge of warmth throughout his body, coupled with a sense of safe surroundings. The room, Alex noticed, had a number of stuffed deer heads and he was lying on a huge comfortable bed. Alex reached for a glass of water, sipped it, and his gaze fell upon an ornate gilded mirror. Recognizing it, he remembered his devoted companion, the likeable Mr. Patel. Alex thought back to how he had joked with Mr. Patel, *"left behind by Queen Victoria no doubt …"*. Painfully turning his head to peer out of the window, Alex saw a familiar view of red and yellow poppy fields in the distance.

The door opened. A young woman with emerald eyes, snow-white skin, and copper shoulder-length hair, wearing a white cotton dress, appeared.

"How are you?" she said.

"What am I doing here?" Alex asked.

"My driver, Mr. Patel brought you here to the Quarters Hotel."

"Who?"

"Mr. Patel, he didn't move from your side until a few moments ago. I believe you know each other."

"Yes, that's right, It's a long story ... how did he find me?" Alex probed.

"A farmer found you … you were caught in a landslide last night. He and Mr. Patel brought you here. Can I get you anything?" she asked.

"May I ask who are you?" Alex probed again.

"Jaleena -- and you?"

"Alex Vadim … pleased to meet you ... what happened? Did I fall?"

"Well yes and no, you slid down the mountain side."

"How far?"

"Sixty feet or so."

"Any bones broken?"

"No, you can get up and walk when you're ready. You're probably just stiff and bruised. Maybe shaken up too? You'll need to rest, but you'll be fine by tonight."

"I guess I lost my cameras?"

"No, they're with Mr. Patel. They're a bit muddy though!"

Impressed by her poise and elegance, he was relieved and grateful that the young woman had concerned herself with his well being. Alex noticed how angelic she looked, how gracefully she moved and how her hair shone against the light of the window as she tucked it behind her ears. Jaleena's eyes were wide and bright and her mouth curled irresistibly into a tentative smile.

"Thanks. Thanks for being here when I woke up." Alex said. *She is quite pretty,* he thought, *she has style.* Alex noticed he had not lost his capacity to be strongly moved by a woman. Jaleena smiled broadly and walked away toward the door. Alex called after her.

"May I invite you for dinner tonight?"

Jaleena turned back and without hesitation said, "Yes, with pleasure. What time?"

"7.30 at the bar? If I can get there," Alex shot back, grinning.

"Agreed."

A few minutes later Mr. Patel walked in shouldering Alex's cameras. The comforting sight of his old companion brought a broad smile to Alex's face. Mr. Patel's elongated moustache, now visibly greying, appeared bushier than he remembered.

"My dear man, how the years have treated you kindly." said Mr. Patel.

Alex noticed a well of tears misting the eyes of this quiet unassuming man, they embraced warmly, then shook hands for several long seconds until Mr. Patel rummaged into his coat pocket, pulled out an enormous white handkerchief and blew his nose noisily.

"Allergies," Mr. Patel mumbled gruffly.

Later that evening during dinner, Alex and Jaleena talked enthusiastically about their passions.

"So why photography, what makes you so keen about it?" Jaleena asked.

Alex thought for a while and then answered. "Few things capture the mind to thought like a great photograph!" he smiled. "You see, still pictures ... decisive images ... can define a moment, or an emotion in ways that films or words alone cannot!"

"So that's why you're here, to find the emotion that defines the moment?" Jaleena asked coquettishly.

"Yes, in a way you're right ... to put emotions to a moment," Alex replied feeling relaxed.

Alex took a good hard look at Jaleena, thinking again how pretty she was. While she listened intently, he spoke with fervour about his work. Jaleena wanted to hear more.

"I've found that there are two kinds of photographers," Alex continued, "the ones who spend most of their time talking about the images they take and their emotional content. Then, there are the photographers who talk non-stop about their fancy cameras and lenses proclaiming their status as *big shots*," he concluded, pouring Jaleena another glass wine.

"So you haven't told me who you work for," she said, holding her glass close to her nose to take in its bouquet.

Alex, turned pale remembering his last conversation with Paris. "CMS, our head office is in Geneva so I'm based there."

"And when you're not?" Jaleena asked licking the edge of her glass.

215

"Well, my hometown is Vaduz in Liechtenstein, a country on the border of Switzerland. I was born there."

"Well that's a coincidence ... because I visited the prince's castle in Vaduz some time back," Jaleena said setting down her wineglass on the wooden table.

"Oh really?" he replied, savouring the red wine. "I've only been once," he said, "on my eighteenth birthday! The monarch invites every citizen to celebrate their eighteenth at the castle!"

"How wonderful! I remember that castle high on the hill where you get to see Austria on one side, Switzerland on another, and Germany just down the valley."

"Yes, that's right." Alex laughed.

Jaleena's month curled into a smile of happiness.

"So how come you speak English like an American?" she asked softly.

"Well, I went to study law at Columbia University in New York, but switched to photojournalism soon after ... against my parents' wishes."

"Why ... or need I ask?" Jaleena said holding out her glass for more.

Alex poured, smiled, slicked back his blond hair and said, "It's my passion, can't you tell? I guess I've always been bit of a rebel so I quit law at Columbia and got into photography whilst in New York."

"And then what?" Jaleena inquired, amused.

"Well, during my second year we were sent to a series of workshops in New Mexico. That's when I hooked up with a couple of mountain-climbers. Actually, they eventually made up the IMAX team which scaled Mt. Everest a few years back. I was on that team."

"What was it like?" she asked fascinated.

"Well that's an interesting question. Everest ... well ... it's bewitching ... beguiling ... and thoroughly intoxicating!"

"What a feat," Jaleena exclaimed intrigued.

"It is, but getting to the summit is an option ... getting down alive ... through the dead zone ... is compulsory!"

"Well that's *very* interesting ... I spent a lot of time in Geneva as a free-lance translator for the United Nations," Jaleena explained with twinkling eyes.

"Oh ... really," Alex replied wondering whether Paris has made it safely up to the palace. "So what *are* you doing *here* in Jammu Kashmir?" he probed.

"I was on my way to Malamar. It's a long story ... do you know Malamar? It's an old palace above Lake Surinsar ... oh, I'm not sure I want to go into it now," she replied avoiding his penetrating blue stare. Jaleena played with her hair for a moment then changed the subject. "And you, what are you doing here?" she inquired.

"Well ... that's a long story too. I got caught in a landslide," Alex teased patting the bandage on his forehead. "Maybe we should get together again and tell each other our long stories," he joked.

"And what now? Do you plan to go back to Europe?" Jaleena probed.

"Yes, well that *was* the plan ... I had thought to leave tomorrow," he responded pouring the last drop into her glass, realising that he might never see Paris again.

Noticing his apparent indecision, Jaleena recognized an opening and smiled, wondering where all this could lead.

"And you?" he asked. "What are your plans ... you'll never make it to Malamar in these conditions, you know," Alex pointed out, hoping for her company back to Srinigar or, he reflected, *anywhere she wanted to go*. He felt unexpectedly calm and oddly at ease with her.

"Yes, I know ... getting there will be difficult ... I've made some plans, but nothing definite," she confessed, thinking about Jovi all alone at the palace.

Alex gathered his thoughts and suggested softly, "Let me give you a ride ... in a day or two. Maybe we'll find enough time to tell each other our long stories!"

14

Dreams

lex Vadim, Explorer, Chief Executive Officer of Cyber Media Solutions; During his brilliant career with CMS spanning twenty-five years, Alex Vadim climbed Everest, covered conflicts in Rwanda, Sierra Leone and The Gulf. Then as chief photographer he went onto cover numerous presidential and congressional campaigns. As well as being assigned to The White House for a number of years to cover major political events ...

Paris closed her *Cyber* magazine. Reading about Alex was something she always enjoyed. After following his career for almost twenty years, she still loved him. She loved the excitement of the unknown, the memories ...

Paris lay on her bed, her lover by her side. She caressed his body and kissed his broad sensual shoulders. She ran her fingers along the small of his back so delicately, as not to awaken him. Paris stroked his hair, gently removed the satin sheet revealing his body and left him lying naked for her eyes to devour. He stirred and said, "Paris, I love you with all my heart, I have always loved you, I will always love you."

Looking at him, she began to write:

I'm lying in my bed under the twirling fan
Catching my dreams, putting them into a bundle
Holding onto my dream catcher
Swirling into slumber
Trying to remember images alight
My very first flight

If only dreams would come true
So that I can adore you
As you are my dream catcher
A place hidden in my heart
Secret passages
Never dark

I'm lying in my bed under the spinning fan
I am dreaming again of flying tonight
And the next thing I know
I am in the air.
Lifted from my bed, parted from my body
Moving alone within the bounds of my room
Floating by the window reaching for the moon
Holding onto my dream catcher

There you are reaching for my fingertips
As I long to hold you and feel the warmth of your lips
Atoms bouncing at the feel of your touch
Did I ever tell you how I have loved so much?
I am swaying and praying as the dream becomes alive
I am creating the potion for our love to survive

I am now drifting in the shadows away from my bed
Letting myself go, so easily led
Don't chase my dreams away
I am your dream catcher
Your powered lights
Don't wake me, let me stay
I am your dream catcher
Your magical nights.

About the Author

Vatsala Virdee was born in Manchester, England to parents originally from Bombay. Having grown up in the Beatles' Britain in the swinging Sixties, and only visiting India during the holidays, at the age of 16 she found herself living in a remote Himalayan hill station after her parents suddenly moved back in the early 70's.

The clash of cultures she experienced in India, particularly at boarding school in Darjeeling, inspired her first novel, Rubies and Rickshaws.

Mrs Virdee has worked with the United Nations in Switzerland since 1981 and lives in Geneva with her husband and their two children.

Printed in the United Kingdom
by Lightning Source UK Ltd.
109303UKS00001B/63